The
–Forty-Acre–
Swindle

Trailblazer Books

The
–Forty-Acre–
Swindle

Dave & Neta Jackson

Story illustrations by
Anne Gavitt

BETHANY HOUSE PUBLISHERS
MINNEAPOLIS, MINNESOTA 55438

Published by Bethany House Publishers
11400 Hampshire Avenue South
Bloomington, Minnesota 55438
www.bethanyhouse.com

Bethany House Publishers is a Division of
Baker Book House Company, Grand Rapids, Michigan.

Printed in the United States of America

Library of Congress Cataloging-in-Publication Data

Jackson, Dave.
    The forty-acre swindle : George Washington Carver / Dave &
Neta Jackson.
        p.   cm. — (Trailblazer books)
    SUMMARY: When his father tries to save the family farm in
Alabama in 1898 by following the advice of George Washington
Carver, fourteen-year-old Jesse struggles to help in his own way.
    ISBN 0–7642–2264–3 (pbk.)
    [1. Farm life—Alabama—Fiction. 2. Afro-Americans—
Fiction. 3. Carver, George Washington, 1864?–1943—Fiction.
4. Alabama—Fiction.] I. Jackson, Neta. II. Title.
PZ7.J132418 Fo   2000
[Fic]—dc21   99–050773

The Turner family in this story is *fictional but typical* of poor black southern farmers who were helped by George Washington Carver's School Wagon and the Farmer's Institutes at Tuskegee Institute, Alabama.

The town of Acorn and its citizens are also fictional, but the prejudicial attitudes and social forces affecting Black Americans around the turn of the century—the cycle of poverty, treatment as second-class citizens, loss of voting rights temporarily gained after the Civil War, the creation of "Jim Crow laws," and the viciousness of lynching as a means of keeping the Negro "in his place"—are, unfortunately, all too true.

All references to George Washington Carver are true representations of his faith, outlook on life, response to injustice, attitudes toward others, and life work.

The phrase "forty acres and a mule": In 1865, at the end of the Civil War, General Sherman issued Special Field Order No. 15, which, among other things, guaranteed forty acres of tillable land per family to former slaves. But President Andrew Johnson rescinded that order, and ultimately, only about 5 percent of the ex-slaves got any land in the first few years of freedom. Most of those who stayed in the South ended up "sharecropping" as tenant farmers.

Note: the words "Negro" and "colored" were common terms of this time period.

Find us on the Web at . . .

trailblazerbooks.com

- Meet the authors.

- Read the first chapter of each book—
  with the pictures.

- Track the Trailblazers around the world
  on a map.

- Use the historical timeline to find out
  what other important events were hap-
  pening in the world at the time of each
  Trailblazer story.

- Discover how the authors research their
  books and link to some of the same
  sources they used where
  you can learn more
  about these heroes.

- Write to the authors.

- Explore frequently asked
  questions about writing
  and Trailblazer books.

LIMITED OFFER:
*Arrange for
Dave and Neta
Jackson to come
to your school or
homeschool
group for a one-
or two-day
writing
seminar.*

CONTENTS

DAVE AND NETA JACKSON are a full-time husband/wife writing team who have authored and coauthored many books on marriage and family, the church, relationships, and other subjects. Their books for children include the TRAILBLAZER series and *Hero Tales* Volumes I, II, III, and IV. The Jacksons have two married children, Julian and Rachel, and make their home in Evanston, Illinois.

Chapter 1

Stranger in Town

THE TOWN OF ACORN popped into view as the big, leggy mule rounded a stand of scrub pines and wild briar, pulling the farm wagon behind him. Sitting beside his father on the driver's seat and lightly holding the mule's reins, Jesse Turner squinted ahead and groaned silently.

Wayne and Udall Buck were sitting on the porch of Dickson's Seed & Feed, their chairs tipped back against the wall of the general store, where they had a good view of anyone coming or going along Acorn's one dusty street.

"Them two," Jesse heard his older brother, Lee, mutter behind him, riding in the bed of the

wagon. "World be a better place if they was to drop off it."

"You jest corral the young'uns, Lee, and don't pay them Buck brothers no mind," warned the boys' father. "Jesse, pull Big Red round to the side."

Jesse hollered, "Gee!" to the mule, then, "Whoa!" Big Red obediently turned right into the shade of the Seed & Feed and stopped.

Scrambling down from the driver's seat, Jesse hung back a little, letting his father go first. No sense being first in the line of fire. He saw that Lee, taking his time about helping nine-year-old Willy and five-year-old Kitty down from the back of the wagon, had the same idea.

"Waal, look who come to town, Udall," smirked Wayne Buck, looking out from beneath a dirty felt hat and a shank of limp, greasy hair. "If'n it ain't our darky neighbor an' his litter o' young'uns." The older of the Buck brothers had a wide red face, with pale stubble on the lower half that never seemed to grow into a beard or get shaved off. His nose was too big for the rest of his face, making his tiny eyes look even smaller.

"Heh, heh, yeah, that right," grinned Udall Buck, revealing several missing teeth. Wayne Buck's "baby brother" was maybe thirty years old, and it was the Turner family's opinion that Udall had something missing upstairs—not that it mattered much. Both brothers seemed to spend more energy swatting flies and bad-mouthing colored folks than working their farm.

"Mornin', Mr. Wayne . . . Mr. Udall," Cecil Turner said with a slight tip of his head, ignoring the brothers' mocking tone.

"Y'all got money to spend today, Cecil? A special 'casion?" Wayne Buck needled.

"Nah," piped up Willy. "We gotta ask Mr. Dickson for more cre—*umph.*" Lee clamped his hand over Willy's mouth and practically dragged the little boy over the doorsill into the store. Jesse quickly herded Kitty after them. When was Willy going to learn to keep his mouth shut about family business! Especially to white folks like Wayne and Udall Buck.

As Jesse's eyes adjusted to the dim coolness of the Seed & Feed, he felt Lee's breath against his ear. "Wouldn't I like to knock the chair legs out from under them Buck brothers and teach 'em a thing or two," the older boy hissed.

Jesse pulled away and looked at his brother in alarm. Black people had been lynched for less in Bullock County, Alabama, even if it was 1898.

"Mornin', Cecil!" came a friendly voice from behind the counter. "Look at how these youngsters are shootin' up! Those boys are almost as tall as you, Cecil. How old are you now, Lee and Jesse?" Harry Dickson, the owner of the Seed & Feed, smiled a welcome as he rolled up his shirt sleeves. It was only nine o'clock in the morning but already getting hot for a Thursday in late May.

Lee didn't answer, and that irritated Jesse. Mr. Dickson had always acted friendly to the Turners, even if he was white. Why did Lee have to be so

11

sullen? Not everybody acted like the Buck brothers.

Jesse felt obligated to answer. "I was fourteen last birthday, Mr. Dickson. Lee here be seventeen now."

"Seventeen. Is that a fact! Well, now, Cecil, did you come back to get more seed, plant those twenty acres you were holding back on? You oughta be able to manage forty acres with the help of these big boys."

Cecil Turner removed his hat. "Oh, they a help, all right," he said. "But . . . like I said las' time I was in, Mr. Dickson, I can't afford no more seed. Truth to tell . . ." Jesse's father twisted the hat in his hands and glanced around the cluttered room nervously. "The wife needs some basic supplies—flour, sugar, salt, cloth to make dresses for the girls. They outgrowin' the old ones. But . . ." The hat was twisted in unrecognizable form by now.

Jesse looked away uncomfortably. Willy and Kitty were studying the fat jars of candy sitting on a side counter. Lee was standing at the window with his back to his father and Mr. Dickson, pretending he wasn't listening to the conversation.

"Well, you know I ain't got no cash right now, Mr. Dickson," his father's voice went on behind him. "Last year's harvest was right poorly. Fact is, uh, I need to ask for more credit."

The silence probably lasted only five seconds, but it felt like five minutes. Then Jesse heard Mr. Dickson clear his throat. "Well, now, Cecil, you know I want to help you whatever way I can. But . . . last year's harvest didn't even pay off your bill from last year. If you keep buyin' on credit, how are you ever gonna get ahead?"

It was awkward, standing still doing nothing. Jesse walked over to his little brother and sister. "You ain't gonna get any candy," he whispered fiercely, "so you might as well stop lookin'."

"Don't hurt nothin' to look," pouted Willy.

The two men's voices had dropped, and Jesse had to strain to hear.

"Well, now, you know my offer still stands, Cecil," Harry Dickson was saying. "I'm willing to buy your place, cancel the debt you owe this store, and give you some cash money besides. Your family can stay on and sharecrop. You can get what you need from the store, no questions asked; we'll just settle up at the end of the year. That way we both share the burden when the harvest is poor like last year."

Sharecrop. Jesse glanced anxiously at his father. Grandpappy George would go straight to his grave today if Papa ever gave away the forty acres George Turner, ex-slave, had gotten with the help of the Freedman's Bureau after the Civil War thirty-some years ago.

"Land . . . land! That's what it mean to be free, owning your own land," Grandpappy George often said, fire burning in his dark eyes. *"Be your own master! Only legacy we got to pass on to these chil'ren. Don't matter* what *happen, son, don't give up the land."*

Jesse's father laughed nervously. "That, uh, mighty generous, Mr. Dickson, sir. I 'preciates it. But you knows how my ol' pappy is about that land.

Would kill him outright if I sold it. No, no, I'm sure we goin' to have a turn for the better. And you know I always pays you first."

"Well, you think about it, anyway, Cecil," said Mr. Dickson. "I'll give you credit today. Dicksons and Turners go a long way back . . . gotta help a man out."

Jesse and Lee exchanged glances. The Dicksons and Turners went a long way back, all right. It was Harry Dickson's father who had owned the huge cotton and tobacco plantation in this part of Bullock County before the war, and Grandpappy George had been a slave on that plantation till he was forty years old. Back then it wasn't "Mr. Dickson," but "Master Dickson." Even Papa had been born a slave, though he was just ten years old when the war ended and the slaves had been freed.

After the war, the U.S. Government had promised "forty acres and a mule" to the former slaves—a promise that few blacks ever realized. But Dickson had been forced to sell off some of his land to get his struggling plantation back on its feet, and the Freedman's Bureau had helped George Turner buy forty acres.

Their grandpappy had been one of the "lucky" ones.

But now that the negotiation for more credit had passed, the tension in Dickson's Seed & Feed seemed to let out a breath. Cecil Turner counted off on his fingers the household goods they needed, while Harry Dickson started to pack them in an empty feed sack.

"Papa," piped up Willy, "can we have some candy?" He was holding the jar of candy sticks. Beside

him, Kitty's eyes pleaded hopefully.

"Put that back," snapped their father. "You know better'n that."

Jesse whacked Willy's arm with the back of his

hand and glared at his little brother. Didn't the boy have any sense at all? Putting Papa on the spot like that in front of Mr. Dickson.

"Well, now," Harry Dickson broke in. His voice sounded like butter on hot corn. "Kids have got to have a bit of a treat now an' then. Go on, Cecil, let the youngsters pick their favorite stick."

Cecil Turner turned to the storekeeper and smiled uncertainly. "Well, now, Mr. Dickson, sir, that's mighty nice, but—"

"No, no, it's no problem," said the storekeeper. He chuckled as Willy selected a green winterberry flavor and stuck it in his mouth. Eyes dancing with excitement, Kitty picked a pink peppermint stick. "No problem at all," Harry Dickson repeated. "I'll just add it to your bill, so you don't even have to worry 'bout it till you come in to settle up."

Jesse saw the smile freeze on his father's face. It was too late now to tell the children to put the candy back. Both were sucking happily on the sticky sweets.

"Now, what else does Jenny need?" prompted Harry Dickson.

"Uh . . . oh yeah, six yards of plain muslin . . ."

Jesse wandered over to the window where Lee was smoldering. He could read his big brother like Mama could read a book, and he knew Lee was angry. Jesse hoped Papa got finished soon so they could go home before Lee popped off and said something that would get them all in trouble.

Something outside caught his eye. "Look at that, Lee," he said.

An odd-looking wagon was rolling into Acorn from the direction of Union Springs, the next largest town ten miles up the road. Two black men Jesse had never seen before were sitting on the driver's seat. The man driving the mule was tall and gangly, maybe thirty years old, wearing a dark, rumpled suit, and sporting a good-sized moustache. Next to him rode another black man, wearing a fancy maroon suit with a starched white shirt and black silk tie, and holding a big satchel on his lap like he was traveling someplace.

Lee glanced out the window. "What of it?" he asked sullenly.

"Never seen those men before," Jesse said in a low voice. "Wonder what they got in that wagon? Look at all those buckets with plants growin' in 'em . . . lots of glass jars, too." A movement caught his eye, accompanied by the sound of two sets of chair legs hitting the wooden porch outside the Seed & Feed with a thud. "Uh-oh."

"What?"

Jesse didn't have to answer. The sound of Wayne Buck's ornery voice carried through the open door.

"You there in the wagon. Stop it right there! What's yo' business here?"

"Yeah," Udall Buck chimed in. "We don't take kindly to strangers round here." The sneer in his voice thickened. " 'Specially no fancy-pants darkies from up North."

The wagon had pulled to a stop a few feet from Dickson's Seed & Feed, and the nattily dressed man in the maroon suit swung down with his big leather satchel.

Jesse felt his father's presence come up behind them. "What's goin' on out there?" said Cecil Turner. He sounded tired.

"I dunno, Papa," said Jesse. "Strangers. The Buck brothers out there givin' 'em a hard time."

Cecil Turner leaned past his boys and peered intently out the window. "Who in—? Why, that's—"

Suddenly the boys' father charged out the door. Following uncertainly, Jesse and Lee—followed by the two youngest Turners, still sucking on their candy sticks—crowded into the doorway of the store. To their surprise, their father and the man in the fancy maroon suit were slapping each other's backs and giving bear hugs. Wayne and Udall Buck stopped swaggering and looked on uncertainly, frowns etched into their red faces.

"Chil'ren!" their father called out. "Come on out here. This ain't no stranger! This here my baby brother . . . back after ten years in Philadelphia. Come on, now. Meet yo' uncle Howie!"

Chapter 2

Woodpile Up in Smoke

JESSE'S JAW DROPPED. This cocky-looking man in the natty suit was their uncle Howie?

The children watched as Howard Turner shook hands with the moustached man on the driver's seat of the wagon and waved good-bye. Papa had often talked about his younger brother Howard, how he had left the farm in 1888 and nearly broke Grandpappy George's heart. But Jesse had been only four years old when his father's brother had gone "up North," and he had only a shadowy memory of the man always referred to as "Uncle Howie."

As the wagon with its strange cargo of glass jars and wooden buckets full of different plants drove on, Cecil Turner

19

picked up his brother's satchel, and the two men started for the porch of Dickson's Seed & Feed. But the Buck brothers, still scowling, stood in their way.

A slight smile twitched on Uncle Howie's lips. "Wayne and Udall Buck . . . bein' friendly, as usual."

Jesse saw his father frown and mutter something under his breath. The smile on Uncle Howie's face disappeared. Slowly removing his hat, he averted his eyes.

"Excuse us, *Mr.* Wayne . . . *Mr.* Udall," said Jesse's father. "Been a long time since we seed my brother, come back for a visit. We'll be gettin' along home now." Then, without another word, he took Howie by the arm, strode over to the Turner wagon, and threw the satchel into the back.

"You really old George's baby boy?" Wayne Buck spit out after them. "Coulda fooled me, all citified up like that in them fancy duds."

"Think you better'n white folks now, don'cha, colored boy, jus' 'cause you been up North," Udall Buck chimed in.

Jesse grabbed Willy and Kitty by the hand and hurried them into the wagon, and Lee hoisted the feed sack of supplies after them. A few minutes later, Cecil Turner had Big Red moving down the road toward the Turner farm at a fast trot.

"Howard Turner, I sure am glad to see you," Cecil said in an exasperated voice, "but if you gon' come back and visit, you gon' have to 'member this is Bullock County, Alabama, and behaves yo'self round white folks."

Uncle Howie shook his head in disgust. "Nothin' changes round here, does it, big brother? Makes me sick, you bowin' and scrapin' to white trash like those Buck brothers."

Lee started to snicker from the back of the wagon bed. Uncle Howie turned around and grinned at him. "You Lee, right?" he said. "Look at you, all growed up. You was just seven years old last time I saw you . . . and Jesse, too. Both you boys done sprout *legs*. Say, where's the baby . . . little girl, if I 'member right. Amanda."

Now it was Jesse's turn to laugh. Twelve-year-old Amanda would have a fit hearing Uncle Howie call her "the baby." "She back home with Mama, helpin' with the washin'. Sent the rest of us packin' with Papa to get us outta her hair." He jerked a thumb at his little brother and sister. "This here's Willy—he's nine—and Kitty. She five."

Uncle Howie winked at Kitty, and the little girl hid her face in Jesse's lap. Uncle Howie turned back to his brother. "How's Pappy?"

"He okay. Gettin' old. You sure gonna be one big surprise. . . . Say, who was that man you was ridin' with? Never seed him round here before."

"Oh, him. Man named Carver . . . he's a professor up in Macon County at Tuskegee Institute—Booker T. Washington's school. Teaches farming. Picked me up just outside Union Springs, gave me a ride."

"Teaches farmin'!" Cecil Turner snorted. "You either *is* a farmer or you *isn't*. Who that Carver think he teachin'?"

Uncle Howie grinned, leaned back, and seemed to drink in the smell of the jasmine and honeysuckle that ran wild along the ditches as the wagon lumbered off the main road and onto a narrower dirt road. "Ahh," he said. "Alabama may not be Paradise, but it sure do smell good, I have to give it that." He straightened up as they passed a field of cotton plants pushing their noses up through the sandy yellow soil. "This still Papa's land?" he asked.

Cecil Turner nodded glumly. "Same forty acres, hangin' on by a thread. Only planted twenty this year—all the seed I could afford."

On the far side of the field, Jesse could hear the rushing waters of Shortcut Creek above the squeaking of the wagon and Big Red's clopping. "Creek's runnin' high this year," he said, wanting to join in the adult conversation.

Uncle Howie listened and nodded. "You better hope that ol' levee holds, or you gonna have one big swamp rather than a cotton field."

"It'll hold," Cecil grunted. "We got sandbags laid up we ain't ever had to use yet."

"Still. You mighta thought the gov'ment give Pappy a better parcel o' land back in '66, given how many years the Turners have worked this land with they blood and they sweat . . . 'stead of this bog."

Cecil Turner just drove on in silence.

As they neared the farm, a black-and-white dog with a patch of black over one eye came racing to meet them, barking joyfully. Jesse grinned. "That there's my dog, Uncle Howie. Name's Patch. He real good at huntin' coons, even though he ain't a hound."

With Patch dancing around his big hooves, Big Red turned into a small lane and stopped beside a small, unpainted house. A thin rope, stretched from the house to a nearby scrub oak, flapped with night-shirts, once-white bedding, and a few shirts and dresses. Suddenly Jesse saw the farm as Uncle Howie—fresh from the big city of Philadelphia—must see it: a gray, ugly house with rusty tin nailed over the holes . . . a smelly pigpen located too near the house, so Papa could plant cotton right up to the yard . . . a broken-down shed that served as a barn for Big Red . . . and the rusty plow sitting in the middle of the dirt "yard." He felt ashamed.

"Jesse, you take care o' Big Red," said his father. "Come on, Howie. Jenny and Pappy sure gonna be surprised."

Taking care of Big Red was Jesse's job. Usually he didn't mind. He had a way with animals—even the pigs. But today he felt a twinge of resentment. It wasn't every day that Uncle Howie showed up from the big city. He wanted to go inside with the rest of the family and hear the talk.

But Big Red was sweaty and needed to be rubbed down. Jesse reluctantly unhitched the wagon and led the mule out of the traces. After giving the mule a drink from the well bucket, Jesse grabbed an old rag and began rubbing off dirt and sweat from the sleek red hide. Big Red shifted his weight to three legs, letting the fourth barely touch the ground, and his eyelids drooped contentedly.

When Jesse finally pushed open the door of the house, Mama was making corn cakes on the top of the wood stove. Jenny Turner wasn't forty yet, and her face still showed traces of her youthful beauty. But backwoods farming in rural Alabama was a hard life, and her hands and feet were rough with calluses. With a practiced hand, she flipped the large corn cake in the hot iron pan, cut it into four pieces, and slid them onto tin plates on the bare wooden table.

"Don't have no butter," she said to Uncle Howie with a wan smile, "but you jus' douse that cake with molasses and you never know the difference." She turned back to the stove, saw Jesse, and eyed the empty woodbox meaningfully.

"Not now, Mama," he pleaded in a whisper. "I'll chop some more straightaway after dinner."

Uncle Howie was sitting next to Grandpappy George at the table, with Willy and Kitty crowded up next to his elbows. Jesse's sister Amanda, a thin girl of twelve, was putting an assortment of cups on the table and filling them with water from a bucket.

". . . lots of jobs in Philly," Uncle Howie was saying. "New factories goin' up ever' day. Think about it, Pappy. Y'all could sell off this dirt farm, pay your debts, move up with me till Cecil and the boys got jobs. Then y'all could get your own place."

Startled, Jesse's eyes darted from face to face around the table. Sell the farm? He saw Lee's eyes glitter with excitement.

Grandpappy George deliberately put a large

forkful of corn cake in his mouth and chewed as he looked at his youngest son. The old man's close-cropped hair was almost white, framing his dark face like a neat cap. He had once been a big man, though now he was stooped and crippled with rheumatism in his joints. No one else spoke as he chewed.

"Sell the land?" he finally asked, his voice tight. "You done forget yo' roots, son. Land is all we got. With land, we is somebody. Without land, we nobody. 'Sides, I was born in Alabama, and I wants to die in Alabama."

Uncle Howie snorted. "Somebody? You think you somebody jus' 'cause you got these pitiful forty acres? Cecil," he said, appealing to his older brother, "what about you? At least think about it."

Cecil Turner just shrugged. "I can't jus' run off to

Philadelphia like you did, Howie. I gots a wife and five kids to support."

Uncle Howie laughed, but the laugh was bitter. "Support? You call living like *this* support?" He jabbed a finger at his brother. "Why, you still eatin' meal and molasses and not much else, just like Pappy did in slavery days. Have you ever voted, Cecil? Have you ever dared speak up to a white man, even when the cotton buyers cheat you? How many black men have they lynched this year in the Southern states—fifty? A hundred? What's so different from slavery times, tell me that?"

All five children stared at Uncle Howie. They'd never heard anyone talk like that to their papa and grandpappy. Silence hung in the room like stiff, starched sheets on washing day.

Jenny Turner's firm voice broke the tension. "Howie Turner, you is family, and you sho' nuff welcome to stay for a visit. But you not welcome to talk to Cecil and yo' pappy that way. These men works hard and I won't have them disrespected in my house. We alive, we still together, and ever' mornin' I thanks the Lord for givin' me breath to see another day. Now, we not complainin' 'bout what we ain't got. So don't go stirrin' up trouble we ain't asked for, you hear?" She stood up and began to clear the tin plates. "Now, come on, these chilluns got work to do. Lee, that field by the road need weedin' . . . . Howie, make yo'self useful and chop weeds with yo' nephew. Jesse, not only that woodbox empty, but the woodpile, too. Go on, now, the lot of you. Get out o' my kitchen."

✧ ✧ ✧ ✧

Jesse straightened his back and angrily wiped the sweat that was running down his face. How come he got stuck stocking the woodpile while Lee got to work with Uncle Howie? It was Friday, the second day of Uncle Howie's visit, and he was *still* chopping wood! Wasn't Willy old enough to swing an ax? Seemed like *he* was nine or ten when he took on this job.

But even as his thoughts smoldered, Jesse knew that chopping wood for the woodbox was one thing, but stocking the woodpile was another. Willy couldn't hitch Big Red to the wagon, go out into the woods to pick up dead wood, and chop fallen trees into pieces he could load into the wagon.

With a sigh of resignation, Jesse threw the last log of loblolly pine, about as big around as his thigh, into the wagon bed and climbed up on the wooden seat. "Git-up!" he said to Big Red, and the wagon lumbered out of the woods, past the levee that held back Shortcut Creek, and down the track that ran alongside the cotton field. Man, he'd sure rather be sinking a line into the creek and catch some fish for supper. At the far end of the cotton field, he could see Lee and Uncle Howie swinging their hoes with an occasional laugh and murmur of voices.

"Uncle Howie sure has taken a shine to Lee," he muttered to Big Red. "Treats him like a man. Well, I may be a few years younger, but I'll show him how a *man* stocks a woodpile."

When Lee and his uncle came in from chopping weeds in the field that evening, Jesse heard Uncle Howie give a low whistle and say, "Man, who put up that stack of firewood 'long that shed? Jenny, you got enough wood there to cook for the entire county rest of the year!"

Jesse grinned in smug satisfaction.

No more had been said about selling the farm and moving to Philadelphia—at least not in the house. But Jesse wondered what Lee and Uncle Howie talked about working out in the field. The two of them seemed as tight as the braids that Mama twisted all over his sister Amanda's head.

Supper was leftover corn cakes from yesterday, fried up with a bit of fatback, and some shriveled sweet potatoes left from last year, boiled up and served with molasses. At the supper table, Uncle Howie told them about his job in a fish-canning factory. It didn't sound like much fun to Jesse, standing in one place all day, packing cold fish you hadn't caught yourself. But he liked hearing about the trolley cars you could ride on for five cents—even the black people!—and the music that happened out in the street in the summertime.

"You go to church up in Philadelphia?" Jenny Turner asked her brother-in-law.

Uncle Howie squirmed. "Well, now, can't say as I do, Jenny," he admitted. "Not ever'body goes up in Philly, not like down here."

"Well, you staying with us, so we 'spects you to go with us come Sunday," she said firmly. Jesse stifled a laugh. Mama sure had a thing about church. Not that he minded. He liked the singing and the preaching and the church dinners once a month. It was the only time they got to see folks, really.

Uncle Howie had been given the straw tick Jesse, Lee, and Willy usually shared out in the lean-to back of the house, so Mama had made pallets for the boys to sleep on in the main room that served as kitchen and sitting room. Jesse woke once in the night when he heard Patch barking . . . probably some old coon. But the barking stopped and it seemed like he'd only just fallen asleep again when he heard Mama banging about the old cast-iron stove, starting the fire for breakfast. He tried to roll over and go back to sleep, but he felt her rough hand shaking his shoulder.

"Jesse," she said. "Get up now. Ain't got enough wood in the woodbox to get us through breakfast, much less the rest o' the day. Go on, now—run out to the woodpile and get me some wood."

Jesse groaned. He had chopped all that wood. Couldn't someone else bring it in and fill up the woodbox? But he knew it wouldn't do any good to protest. Rubbing his eyes, he opened the sagging front door of the house to a gray, cloudy dawn and stumbled across the dirt yard toward the shed.

Then he stopped and rubbed his eyes again.

The woodpile was gone. Every last stick of it . . . gone. As if the whole woodpile had gone up in smoke.

Chapter 3

Levee Down!

WHAT DO YOU MEAN, GONE? If you playin' some kind o' joke—" Jenny Turner stuck the last piece of wood from the woodbox into the fire in the stove and banged the round stove lid shut. She clearly had no patience for foolishness this early in the morning.

"I'm not jokin', Mama! Come look! The whole woodpile is gone!"

Jesse dashed back outside, still not believing his eyes, followed by his mother. Hearing the ruckus, the whole Turner family was soon standing in the dirt yard, staring at the side of Big Red's shed, which was bare as a newborn baby.

Uncle Howie said something under his breath.

"How could a whole woodpile jus' get up and walk away, Papa?" little Kitty asked, wide-eyed.

"Woodpile didn't walk away," Cecil Turner said tightly. "Somebody done walk away *with* it."

Grandpappy George shuffled out of the house, shrugging an arm through his suspenders. "Where that good fer nothin' dog? How could somebody come in this here yard and us not hear the dog?"

Suddenly Jesse remembered the barking in the night. Had something happened to— "Patch!" he called anxiously. "Here, boy! Here, Patch!"

To his relief, a bundle of black-and-white fur wiggled out from under the rusty plow and came bounding over to the little group. While Jesse buried his face in the dog's fur, Lee walked over to the plow, reached under it, and pulled out a huge knucklebone gnawed almost clean. "Look like 'somebody' bribed the dog," Lee snorted.

"Mercy!" said Jenny Turner. "Wastin' that big, meaty bone on a dog. Woulda made 'nuff soup for two days." She turned on Jesse. "Well, thieves or no thieves, I needs wood to do my cookin'. Looks like you gots yo' Saturday work cut out. Lee, help yo' brother. Howie can help Papa today."

"Mama!" Jesse wailed. "Took me two days to cut all that wood! Ain't my fault somebody stole it!"

"He right, Mama," said Lee. " 'Stead o' cuttin' more wood, we should go find who stole it and get it back!"

Cecil Turner whirled on his boys. "You won't do

no such thing! You hear me? That a sure way to get in a heap o' trouble. Now, do like yo' mama says. Rustle up some wood for the breakfast fire, then take the wagon and load it up from the woods."

"You jus' gonna let somebody come in here and steal your firewood and do nothin' 'bout it?" Uncle Howie challenged.

Cecil jabbed a finger at his brother. "You stay out o' this, Howie. Some things is more important than a few sticks o' wood."

"*What's* more important, big brother?" shouted Howie. "It ain't the wood I'm thinkin' 'bout. It's 'bout not lettin' people walk all over you!"

"Watch yo' tongue, Howie Turner," Jenny jumped in. "There be young'uns here. 'Sides, Cecil be right. Good Book say we s'posed to turn the other cheek. Now, come on, all o' you. Wood ain't gonna show up with us jus' standin' here."

Two hours later, Jesse and Lee were following the old wagon track into the woods behind Big Red. "What you think happen to that wood, Lee?" Jesse said.

"I got a good idea," Lee muttered. "Wanna find out?"

Jesse looked at him sharply. "What you mean?"

Lee pointed. "Take that track goin' back through the woods that way. It come out on the road near Thomas Tagoosa's place."

"You think Thomas took our wood?" Jesse asked, shocked. Thomas Tagoosa was their nearest neighbor, a man who kept pretty much to himself, living alone in a shack that barely kept the weather out and sharecropping a few acres for Harry Dickson.

"Nah, not Thomas," snorted Lee. "But who live just beyond Thomas's place?"

Jesse stared at his brother. Wayne and Udall Buck lived a couple hundred yards farther down that same road.

"Who else?" shrugged Lee.

"But we can't go drive the wagon up they lane!" Jesse protested. "They run us off with a shotgun."

"Let's just go see."

As Big Red and the wagon broke out of the trees and pulled out on a narrow dirt road, the boys saw Thomas Tagoosa's shack. "Pull in there," said Lee. Jesse yelled, "Haw!" and the mule obediently turned into the small clearing that was Tagoosa's homestead.

Thomas Tagoosa came out of his shack, smoking a pipe. His straight black hair was pulled back from his broad, dark face in a ponytail, testimony to his mixed Negro and Creek Indian heritage. "Howdy, Jesse . . . Lee," he said. "Do somethin' for you boys?"

Lee jumped down off the wagon. "Can we leave our wagon here for 'bout half an hour, Thomas?"

The middle-aged man eyed them suspiciously. "You boys s'posed to be workin'?"

Jesse and Lee looked at each other, then found themselves telling Thomas about the stolen wood. Their neighbor frowned. "I'll look after yo' wagon . . . but you boys be careful. Them Buck brothers got a mean streak. Won' take kindly to you snoopin' 'bout."

Moments later Jesse and Lee had scurried across
the road and were making their way through the
underbrush. A light drizzle started, masking their
footsteps. Crouching down behind a tangle of wild

brier, the boys peered through the bushes at the Buck brothers' shack. Smoke drifted out of the tin chimney on top of the roof, and all along one side of the shack stood a big woodpile of freshly cut wood.

✧ ✧ ✧ ✧

"That *our* firewood, Papa!" Lee stormed when they got back that evening with a wagonload of foraged wood. "Not a chance them lazy Buck brothers cut it theyselves. We oughta go and demand it back."

"What I *oughta* do is whip you boys good for disobeyin' me," Cecil Turner snapped. "What good it do to find out who took it? You think those Buck brothers just gonna hand that wood back?"

"*Take* it back durin' the night, then," Jesse muttered. His muscles screamed with another day of dragging and chopping wood. "Or go tell Mr. Dickson. *He* could make 'em give it back."

Their father's jaw muscles worked back and forth as he tried to control himself. "How you goin' to prove that our wood?" he said finally. "It our word against theirs. An' since when has anyone in this county taken the word of a colored man over a white man? You go accusin' them Bucks o' stealin', an' you find yo'self swingin' at the end of a rope."

"Cecil!" his wife cried. "Don't talk like that in front o' the young'uns."

"Well, that be the end of it, then," said the boys' father. "Go put that mule away, Jesse, an' wash up for supper."

35

The drizzle had stopped, but the day had stayed gray and cool. Jesse noticed that the sky was darker than usual to the west. He figured they were going to get a good storm before the night was out. "Just as well," he muttered angrily to Big Red as he led the mule into the shed, past the pile of old sandbags, and began rubbing the mule's hide hard with the old rag. "Rain'll keep them Buck brothers home 'stead o' out doin' they mischief."

He took longer than usual to stable the mule, still angry about all his chopped wood sitting over at Wayne and Udall Buck's place. When he finally slipped into the house, the family was at the table eating rice and gravy, and Uncle Howie was talking.

"Why not let the boy come with me, Cecil?" he was saying. "He old enough to work in the factory, make him some real money."

"Now, don't go puttin' ideas in the boy's head."

"But I want to go, Papa!" said Lee.

"You stay out of this, Lee."

Jesse slipped into his place at the table, but no one took any notice.

"Now, Cecil, think on it," said Uncle Howie. "What kinda future there be for the boy here? If you want to hold on to this miserable farm, that your business. But let the boy have a chance—"

Grandpappy George broke in. "Farm is all I got to leave my gran'chil'run. Lee, here, be the firstborn."

"I don't want it," Lee muttered.

"I'm not askin' you what you want!" snapped Cecil Turner. "Point is, I needs both you and Jesse to

36

help me with th' cotton, an' I'll thank yo', Howie, not to start messin' with what we gots to do here."

"You a stubborn ol' goat, Cecil Turner," said Uncle Howie. "Jus' 'cause you ain't never been out o' Bullock County—"

Jenny Turner stood up abruptly. "I won't have my husband disrespected at his own table," she said stiffly. "Howie, I think it's time for you to go."

A sudden, uncomfortable silence sifted into the room. Then Uncle Howie slowly rose from his chair. "You right, Jenny. I've overstayed my welcome. I'll jus' get my bag . . . got a few friends I'd like to see 'fore I head back up to Philadelphia. Pappy . . ." Howie looked at the old man, and his voice got husky. "You take care o' yo'self, now, hear?"

"Mama," whimpered little Kitty. "Ain't Uncle Howie goin' to church with us tomorrow?"

"Hush," Mama said.

Within five minutes Uncle Howie had packed his bag and was gone.

✧ ✧ ✧ ✧

Jesse pulled the thin blanket over his head and tried to shut out the loud voices from the main room of the house. The rest of the children had been sent off to bed, but Lee was mad.

"You don't care if I amount to anything!" his older brother was shouting. "Uncle Howie givin' me a chance to get outta this mudhole, but no! You want me to pick cotton the rest o' my life. How that dif'rent than slave times, tell me that?"

Thunder rumbled in the distance. Jesse's feelings sloshed around inside him like a bucket of gritty water from the well. He was glad Papa hadn't let Lee go with Uncle Howie—what if he went away and didn't come home for ten years, like Uncle Howie? Why did Lee want to go to Philadelphia anyway? Working inside a smelly factory all day long . . . nothing special about that. Why, nothing beat fishing Shortcut Creek on a hot summer afternoon.

At the same time, Jesse was jealous that Uncle Howie wanted *Lee* to go to Philadelphia with him. Why not him? Or at least both of them?

The voices in the other room were heating up. "I'm almost growed," Lee was saying. "If I take it in my mind to go after Uncle Howie, ain't nothin' you can do to stop me!"

"That right?" Papa was shouting now. "You try it, boy, an' I'll come after you so quick, you won't know me from a whirlwind!"

Another rumble of thunder, closer now, and rain began to patter on the roof. Lee came stomping into the lean-to, banging the door behind him, and Jesse could hear him breathing heavily in the dark. Jesse felt scared. Would his brother really run off? A flash of lightning showed Lee leaning against the small, cracked pane of glass that served as a window in the lean-to, anger etched on his face.

But just then a deafening thundercrack, followed by a roar of rain on the roof, reassured him. Lee wouldn't be going anywhere in a storm like this.

Comforted, Jesse rolled over on the straw tick and fell asleep.

✧ ✧ ✧ ✧

Pounding . . . pounding . . .

Jesse sat straight up in bed and listened. The storm was quiet. But he heard his father's feet hit the floor and then the front door open.

"The levee's broken!" a voice shouted. "We gotta plug it now!" The voice belonged to Thomas Tagoosa.

"Lee! Jesse!" boomed their father's voice. "Get outta that bed and come quick! We gotta plug the levee!"

The door to the lean-to banged open, and their father's big frame filled the doorway. Jesse reached over to shake Lee on the pallet beside him.

But Lee was gone.

Chapter 4

Pick-Up Sticks

JESSE RAN FOR THE SHED. The rain had stopped, but the trees still dripped and the dark night hung damp and heavy over the stretch of mud between the house and shed. He knew Papa was furious that Lee was missing. Gone—right when he was needed. Not only gone, but Papa couldn't go after him because they had to load up the sandbags and get out to the levee.

Jesse's feet skidded in the thick mud. When had Lee slipped out? Where did he go? How did he—? He stopped, his hand on the latch of the shed door. What if . . . what if Lee had taken Big Red, and they couldn't go plug up the levee!

Sucking in his breath, Jesse lifted

the latch and slowly swung open the door. The shed was pitch dark . . . but a familiar snuffle and *thump* told him Big Red was still in his stall.

Letting out his breath in relief, he saw the dark shadow of the mule's head swing toward him curiously. "Sure am glad to see you, you ol' mule," he said affectionately, sliding his hand along the mule's rump. He stopped, startled, then ran his hand down the mule's leg.

Big Red was wet. Wet and muddy.

Jesse felt confused. He *knew* he had rubbed the mule down last night when he and Lee got back with the load of foraged wood. And even if he hadn't, Big Red would be dry by now.

"Jesse!"

His father's voice shook him into action. Grabbing the mule's harness off its peg, he led Big Red outside and backed him into the wagon traces. By the time he had the mule hitched, Papa and Thomas Tagoosa were hauling sandbags out of the shed and loading them into the back of the wagon. Mama and Amanda appeared and began grabbing sandbags, too.

The sandbags were heavy, and it took time to load the wagon. Too much time. How long had Shortcut Creek been flooding their field?

"Where to?" Cecil Turner yelled at Thomas Tagoosa as the last sandbag was loaded.

"Yo' last field next to my place!" Thomas shouted back. "Where Shortcut Creek takes a bend by that stand o' pine forest."

Mama sent Amanda back inside the house to stay with Willy and Kitty, then climbed in the back with Thomas. But as Jesse gathered up the reins he heard a voice call out, "Wait!" All heads swiveled to see Grandpappy George making a beeline for the wagon.

"Pappy!" Cecil protested. "I don't want you lifting no—"

"Move over," Grandpappy ordered Thomas, who was sitting on the tailgate. "Somebody give me a hand here."

Jesse had to grin as his papa and Thomas Tagoosa gave the old man a hand into the wagon bed. "Git up!" he yelled at Big Red and slapped the mule into a trot. No, sir. George Turner wasn't likely to sit home by the stove if something was threatening his land.

The rain started again as Jesse turned Big Red into the narrow lane that ran along the newly planted cotton field. Not heavy, just a steady drizzle. "Pull up as close as you can to the levee!" Thomas shouted. "The break ain't far in—'bout ten, fifteen yards."

Jesse swung Big Red into the field and called, "Whoa!" He watched as Papa and Thomas scrambled up on the levee, feeling their way in the dark to where Thomas had found the break. In a few minutes they were back.

"Water pourin' through a hole size o' a tree log," said Papa grimly. "Jenny, you stay on the wagon and push sandbags to the back best as you can. Jesse . . . Pappy, you pass the bags along. Thomas and me, we'll shore up the break on the levee."

Jesse hefted a bag onto his shoulder, staggered a

little under its weight, then slogged ankle deep in dirt and water into the field. A break as big as a log? How could that be? Papa made him and Lee walk the levee along Shortcut Creek every couple of weeks, and they hadn't seen anything that looked like trouble. In some places the levee was a natural bank; in others, like here at the end of this field, the levee had been strengthened with logs and sod and brush that had grown together like a wall. Even with as much rain as they'd been having, the levee should have held.

He passed the sandbag off to Grandpappy and slogged back to the wagon for another one. On the wagon, Mama pushed sandbag after sandbag to the tailgate, where Jesse slid them one at a time onto his shoulder and trudged back to his grandfather. Even as his eyes adjusted to the dark night, he could barely see his father and Thomas up on the levee.

The little crew worked without talking, and Jesse was alone with his thoughts. Should he tell Papa about Big Red being wet and muddy in the shed? No . . . Papa had enough to worry about, with Lee being gone and all. Sure was strange, though. And how long had this field been flooding? Even if they got the levee dammed up, they might not be able to save the new cotton plants.

On one of his trips back to the wagon, his mama broke into his thoughts. "How yo' grandpappy doin', Jesse?"

Jesse shrugged. "Guess he all right. He ain't said nothin'."

Jesse had no idea how long they'd been working when he realized night had given way to a damp gray dawn. It was Sunday morning.

"That's it!" Mama called out, indicating the wagon was empty.

"All right!" Papa yelled back. "Thomas and me gonna shift some bags round up here."

Done at last. Jesse's muscles felt like they'd been tightened with a winch, but he waded through the field toward the levee to see where the break had been. But as he drew closer to the levee, he noticed something strange—a long gash running *across* the rows of cotton, filled with water, as if something had been dragged across the field. He hadn't seen it before in the dark, but now in the light . . .

Instead of climbing up on the levee, he turned and followed the gash through the soft mud. It came out of the field and went into the stand of sweet-smelling pines. Puzzled, Jesse squished his way through the soggy mat of pine needles . . . and then stopped.

A muddy log lay at the end of the gash, hidden in the trees. Jesse peered closer at the ground. Big hoofprints sank into the ground along the path of the gash and continued on beyond the log.

But the strangest thing of all was a leather harness strap hooked around the front end of the log, which looked like it had snapped off at a weak point.

Jesse stared at the log and the harness strap. And then he knew what he was looking at.

Someone had *pulled* that log out of the levee.

Cecil and Jenny Turner, Thomas Tagoosa, and Grandpappy George all stood with Jesse staring at the log and the broken strap. "Somebody pull that log out, like pullin' out a stick from Willy's game o' Pick-Up Sticks, making the whole pile fall down," Jesse's mama murmured, shaking her head.

Papa said nothing, but Jesse could see the muscles in his jaw working. Nobody asked, "Who did it?" They all had a pretty good idea who.

"Woodpile's one thing, Cecil," said Thomas Tagoosa. "Bad joke. But this . . . this yo' *livin'*." The unspoken words, *"An' what you gonna do 'bout it?"* hung between them.

"I know," said Cecil between clenched teeth. "What you think, Pappy?"

Grandpappy George didn't answer. Jesse looked at his grandfather and realized the old man was breathing funny. One hand was stretched out and pressed against a pine tree, letting the tree hold him up.

"Grandpappy?" Jesse said sharply. "Papa! Somethin's wrong with Grandpappy!"

"Oh, mercy, it be his heart," said Mama.

"I *knowed* I shouldn't o' let him come!" Papa said. "Quick! We got to get him a doctor!"

The men sprang into action. Half carrying, half dragging the old man, they managed to get him into the back of the empty wagon. Jesse's father leaped into the driver's seat and yelled at Big Red. The mule

snorted and pulled, but the wagon wheels were sunk in the water and mud of the flooded field and barely moved.

"Push it!" yelled Papa. Jesse and Thomas Tagoosa jumped off and leaned their shoulders against the big spoked wheels. Slowly the wagon began to move as Big Red snorted and pulled and blew.

As the wagon wheels finally rolled onto more solid ground, Jesse and Thomas leaped back on the wagon, and Big Red took off at a furious trot.

Mama was holding Grandpappy's head in her lap. A sudden fear gripped Jesse. Was Grandpappy going to die? It was all too much. Lee running off... somebody deliberately flooding their field... and now, Grandpappy... *Oh, God, don't let my grandpappy die,* he pleaded silently. *Please, God, please...*

"Jesse?" A raspy whisper caught Jesse's attention. He realized his grandfather was motioning to him. Jesse scrambled over on the wagon bed and leaned close to the old man's face. "What, Grandpappy?"

Grandpappy George reached out a hand and pulled Jesse's ear down to his mouth. "I gots a sock... 'neath a floorboard under mah bed," he gasped in a whisper, "... ta pass on ta mah gran'chil'run. But..." The old man clutched Jesse's shirt. "Lee gone. You keep it, Jesse... keep it for th' land."

The old man sank back onto his daughter-in-law's lap. "Shh, shh," Jenny hushed. "Don't talk, Pappy." She looked at Jesse strangely. "What he sayin' to you, son?"

Jesse just shook his head and shrugged. A sock? What was Grandpappy talking about?

✧ ✧ ✧

When they got to the house, there was a hurried consultation about what to do next. Grandpappy was still short of breath and complaining of chest pain. The closest doctor was in Union Springs, ten miles away. Mama didn't think Grandpappy could stand the trip, but Papa argued that it would take twice as long to go get a doctor and bring him back, and that might be too late!

Finally they decided to leave Jesse at home to look out for Amanda and the two younger children while Papa and Mama took Grandpappy in the wagon to Union Springs.

"Ain't we goin' to church this mornin', Jesse?" Kitty whimpered as the wagon turned out of their yard and headed toward Union Springs.

"Where Lee at?" Willy wanted to know.

"Jesse, I'm scared," Amanda said, her face streaked with tears.

Jesse was scared, too, but he tried to act brave. "Come on, now, we gotta eat somethin'," he said. "I'll make a fire in the stove, Manda, if you can make us some corn cakes or somethin'. No, Kitty, we ain't goin' to church this morning, but . . . I 'spects folks at church will pray for Grandpappy when they hear why we not there."

Picking his way through the mud to the pile of foraged wood, Jesse got the ax out of the shed and began to chop. *Lee. Good question, Willy.* Where *was* Lee? Would Papa go looking for Lee in Union Springs? That's where Uncle Howie would have to catch the train for Philadelphia.

Chop . . . chop. The events of last night turned over and over in Jesse's mind as he worked. Uncle Howie leaving . . . the argument between Lee and his parents . . . the thunderstorm . . . the levee breaking . . . discovering that Lee was gone . . . finding Big Red wet and muddy in the shed . . .

Jesse straightened and a frown deepened on his forehead. Why *was* Big Red wet and muddy in the middle of the night?

A horrible thought crowded to the front of Jesse's mind. He pushed it away, but it pushed back and demanded attention.

Had Lee *used Big Red last night to pull that log out of the levee?*

Chapter 5

Burning Money

B Y SUNDOWN ON SUNDAY, Mama and Papa still had not returned. All day long Jesse had worried about Lee. Why would Lee pull the log out of the levee? But if he didn't, why was Big Red all wet and muddy?

It didn't make any sense. Unless... A thought crossed Jesse's mind as he took a bucket of table leavings out to the pigpen and stood watching the scrawny hog noisily stick its nose in the wooden trough. Maybe... maybe Lee *wanted* the cotton crop to fail so Papa would sell out and go to Philadelphia, like Uncle Howie said.

As twilight deepened under still-leaden skies, Jesse lit the one oil lamp.

"Read us the Bible, like Mama does," Kitty demanded, pushing the big book onto Jesse's lap after their meager supper of cold corn cakes and sweet tea. Jesse was tired. It was hard work keeping the stove fire going to take the chill out of the house, mucking out Big Red's stall in the shed, feeding the pig, helping Amanda keep track of Willy and Kitty, hauling water from the well, wiping up the mud they tracked into the house all day, and answering questions till he lost count. But he opened the big book and tried to read a psalm to his brother and sisters.

"The . . . Lord . . . is . . . my . . . shepherd," he read slowly. "I . . . shall . . . not . . . want."

Papa couldn't read, but Mama had gone to school for two years when she was a girl, in a little log school for colored children. But the colored families around Acorn couldn't afford to keep paying a teacher back then, and they weren't allowed to attend the white school, so that was all the schooling she had.

The little log school had never opened again.

But Mama was determined to teach her children to read. The only book the Turners had was an old Bible, but all of them except Kitty could read some.

"What's that?" Willy asked suddenly.

"What?" said Jesse.

"Sounds like the wagon!" All four children tripped over themselves getting to the door and tumbling outside into the late evening twilight.

Big Red had just turned into the yard pulling the wagon. Mama and Papa sat together on the high seat in front. But . . . where was Grandpappy?

The children stood like clumps of clay as Papa said, "Whoa!" and then helped Mama down from the wagon seat. Without a word, Papa went around to the back of the wagon, and the children followed slowly, their eyes wide with dread.

In the back of the wagon sat a long, plain wooden box.

"Grandpappy gone home to be with Jesus," whispered Mama. She put an arm around Kitty and Amanda. "He at rest now. But we gonna miss him . . . we sho' gonna miss him."

❖ ❖ ❖ ❖

The next day Papa went to see Deacon Little about doing a funeral for Grandpappy George, Tuesday at the latest. Then he and Thomas Tagoosa spent the rest of the day digging a six-foot hole in the little cemetery in back of the Mount Zion Missionary Baptist Church.

Late Tuesday afternoon Jesse hitched up Big Red and brought the wagon up to the house. Mama and Papa came out dressed in their Sunday best, though the old black suit and Mama's dress had seen better days. All the children wore clean clothes, but not shoes. Shoes were only for wintertime.

Every colored family around Acorn showed up at Mount Zion for George Turner's funeral. Everybody knew George. His story was every family's story: once a slave, born right here in Bullock County; trying to eke a living from the red-and-yellow clay soil, planting cotton, picking cotton; either share-cropping or trying to hold on to little plots of land; living hand-to-mouth, raising a family, and hoping for a better day tomorrow.

After the crying and singing, an old man everyone called "Uncle Digs" got up. "George and me, we was both born on the Dickson plantation," he quavered. "I 'member his mammy—she was a pray-er, she was. . . ."

That would be my great-granny Emma, thought Jesse.

"Emma Turner would takes us young'uns into th' woods ta gather firewood, an first thing we knowed she'd be down on her knees behind a stump, a-prayin' an' wipin' her eyes with th' corner of her apron. Always prayin' her babies be set free someday, an' that th' Lord help 'em ta hold on." The old man's voice quavered again. "I 'spects now that George has joined her up in heaven, she still be a-prayin' for all her gran'babies."

A woman's voice broke out with the familiar song, "Put yo' han' on th' plow, hold on!" and the little pine-board church seemed to dance on its shaky foundation.

After the singing and testifying, Deacon Little preached a long-winded sermon on "preparing to meet thy Maker." And then Papa and Thomas Tagoosa and some of the other men carried the wooden coffin out to the little graveyard behind the church.

Everybody took turns shoveling dirt on top of Grandpappy's coffin once it had been lowered into the grave. As Jesse picked up the shovel, he felt

soaked in sadness. He was going to miss Grandpappy
George. But he didn't have a hard time believing
Grandpappy was in heaven with Jesus. Often in the
evening, after the day's work was done, Grandpappy
would sit in a chair outside the door of the house,
singing some of the slave spirituals his own mama
had taught him. "All th' tears gonna be wipe away
someday," he'd say to the children who hung around
nearby listening to Grandpappy sing. "If it don't
happen here first, at least Jesus done fix us a man-
sion up in heaven."

As the clods of red dirt filled up the grave, Jesse
felt another layer of sadness overwhelm the first.
Lee was gone, too. And Lee didn't know that
Grandpappy was dead.

Jesse made a sudden decision. He couldn't tell

Papa about Big Red being wet and muddy the night the levee broke. If he admitted his worry that maybe Lee had pulled the log out of the levee, Papa might blame Lee for Grandpappy's death.

❖ ❖ ❖ ❖

Wednesday morning Jesse stood with Papa and Thomas Tagoosa, looking at the soggy cotton field. The water from the break in the levee had sunk into the ground, but more than half the young plants had been washed out, their roots exposed and withered by two days of sun.

"Don't know what I'm gonna do," said Papa heavily.

The field was almost a total loss. If they could

have replanted the dislocated shoots before the roots dried out, some might have been saved. But Grandpappy George's death had killed that possibility.

The big man turned to his neighbor. "Thomas, how come you even thought to check out the levee that night?"

"Heard a mule goin' through the woods past my house. Thought it might be you—goin' to check the levee 'cause of the bad storm. So I put on my slicker and headed for the levee. 'Cept you wasn't there. Nobody was. But I could hear Shortcut Creek bustin' through the levee and fillin' up yo' field."

Jesse pricked up his ears. "A mule? Did you hear which way it went out on the road?" It was a risky question. One direction led to the Buck brothers' shack; the other to the Turner farm.

Thomas shrugged. "Can't rightly say. Thought I was wrong about hearin' the mule—till we found that pulled log. But my guess is it was headed thataway." He jerked a thumb in the general direction of Wayne and Udall Buck's place.

Cecil Turner's eyes narrowed at the implication. Then he said abruptly, "Ain't no way round it. I got to go talk to Harry Dickson again, see if he give me some more cottonseed on credit. Jesse, you come 'long—but keep yo' mouth shut if we see those Buck boys."

❖ ❖ ❖ ❖

To Jesse's relief, the two chairs on the porch of Dickson's Seed & Feed were empty. Was it only a week since they'd last been to Dickson's store? So much had happened. Uncle Howie had come and gone . . . Grandpappy had died . . . Lee was gone.

"Mornin', Cecil. Mornin', Jesse," called out Mr. Dickson from behind the counter where he was stocking his shelves. "Say, Cecil, I sure was sorry to hear about your pappy. An' what's this 'bout Shortcut Creek bustin' out of the levee and drowning your bottomland?"

Jesse snorted to himself. No secrets around Acorn. Did Mr. Dickson also know that Lee had run off? How much was his father going to tell him?

"Waal, that's what I come to see you 'bout, Mr. Dickson, sir," said Cecil politely, removing his hat. "I need to buy more cottonseed on credit."

Harry Dickson frowned. "That field's too wet to plant now, Cecil."

Cecil Turner nodded patiently. "I know that. Gonna have to turn under some o' mah acres lying fallow."

"Thought you said those acres weren't producin' so good."

Jesse could see his father's facial muscles tense. "Ain't got no choice now. Done lost mah best bottomland. But I got to plant somethin' if I hope to pay you what I owe you come harvest an' feed mah family this winter."

The storekeeper wagged his head from side to side. "Cecil, it sure does look like you've had a string o' bad luck, an' I surely do sympathize. But . . . look at it from my point of view. Cottonseed costs money—and frankly, I'm not likely to see it come back to me come harvest." He shook his head again. "I'm sorry, Cecil. I just can't give you any more credit—not without some kind of collateral."

Jesse's father looked confused. "Collateral?"

"You know—something that guarantees I'm goin' to get my money back if you can't pay me."

Cecil Turner twisted his hat. Finally he said, "Jesse, step outside. I got to talk business with Mr. Dickson, here."

Now it was Jesse's turn to be confused. His father always talked business in front of his boys. *That how they learn,"* he had told his wife.

Jesse went outside and thought about sitting in the chairs on the porch, then thought better of it and sat on the edge of the porch, dangling his legs and kicking the dust of Acorn's street. He'd been waiting maybe ten minutes when his father came striding out the front door.

"Did you get the seed, Papa?" he asked eagerly.

"I got it," said Cecil Turner grimly. "We pick it up round back."

✧ ✧ ✧ ✧

Jesse had been surprised that Papa had gotten twice as much seed as he'd used to plant the bottom-land. "Needed it," Papa explained curtly. "Gotta plant twice as much in that tired ol' soil up on top o' Sugar

Hill to get the same crop. Wind an' rain done blow the topsoil off."

Jesse didn't know why Sugar Hill was called Sugar Hill—probably because the Dickson plantation had planted sugarcane there years ago.

"But, Papa," Jesse protested. "Those fields ain't ready to plant. Still got ol' dried stalks from last year's crop."

"I know that!" snapped Cecil. "We gonna burn it off. But first we gotta plow a firebreak round the edge of both fields. That yo' job first thing tomorrow."

It occurred to Jesse that with Lee gone, he was going to end up with twice the work, and for the first time he felt angry with his brother.

"He jus' selfish, that what he is," Jesse complained to Big Red the next day as the mule leaned against the harness and dragged the plow back and forth around the edges of the tired fields on Sugar Hill. Jesse's father came along behind, gathering up the dried stalks cut by the plow and tossing them into the field to be burned.

"That wide enough!" Cecil finally called to his son. The afternoon sun had already sunk behind the oak trees below Sugar Hill. "We'll burn it off tomorrow."

Father and son arrived at Sugar Hill the next day when the morning breeze had died down so the fire would be easier to control. They'd brought a metal bucket of coals from the cast-iron stove and several "torches" made from pine knots full of sap. Jesse gathered a pile of dried stalks from last year's meager cotton crop to start the fire. But his heart wasn't in it. What good would all this work do? Last year's crop had been disappointing. What made Papa think it was going to do any better this year?

Cecil Turner pulled a burning pine knot torch out of the bucket of coals and said, "All right, now, stand back."

"Stop, brother!" called out a high tenor voice.

Startled, father and son whirled around to see a tall, lanky black man climbing the dirt track that led up Sugar Hill. But there was something vaguely familiar about him. . . .

"Papa!" said Jesse. "That the school man what gave Uncle Howie a ride from Union Springs last week."

Papa frowned and waited till the tall stranger had come up alongside the firebreak. The man was dressed in the same rumpled black suit he'd been wearing before, his full moustache framing his mouth, and his shaggy brows and wrinkled forehead giving him a constant worried look.

"Mighty glad I came along when I did," puffed the stranger after his quick climb. "You burn that field, my brother, and it'll be just like burning off the outside dollar bills on a roll of greenbacks!"

Jesse stared. What was the man talking about? Was this some kind of foreign language?

"Oh—excuse me," said the man, extending his hand. "My name is Carver. George Washington Carver at your service. I head up the Agriculture Department at Tuskegee Institute."

Chapter 6

Signed in Blood

CECIL TURNER SHOOK PROFESSOR CARVER'S HAND, but Jesse noted there was distance in his gaze—the kind of distance his father usually reserved for white folks. *"Don't let 'em know what you're really thinking. Be polite, but don't let down your mask."*

"What you tryin' to say ... Carver, is it? 'Bout burnin' dollar bills."

"Exactly!" said Carver. He squatted down and let some of the pale soil sift through his fingers. "This poor ol' soil is tired and hungry. Been feeding ol' King Cotton for years, till it just doesn't have anything left." He stood up again. "Plow that roughage under! Don't let it go up in smoke! Those old plant stalks have got some good nutrients

hidden away. Let 'em decay and enrich your soil."

Cecil Turner pursed his lips. "That right?"

"And another thing, my good man," Carver went on. "I see you've got cottonseed in your wagon, ready to plant. Let me make a suggestion that will change your fortune: cowpeas."

"Cowpeas!" Jesse snorted. Now he *knew* the man was talking a foreign language. No one grew cowpeas around Acorn. There wasn't any market for them. Cotton—that was the cash crop in Bullock County.

George Carver smiled. "That's right. You see, young man, God created a wonderful relationship between soil, plants, and animals—that includes people, mind you. Animals and people feed on the plants, the plants feed on the soil—but what does the soil feed on?"

"Fertilizer!" Jesse blurted, feeling a bit smug. He'd seen big bags of fertilizer in Dickson's Seed & Feed.

The professor nodded. Then he added wryly, "But I suppose you folks have noticed that commercial fertilizer costs a lot of money."

Cecil Turner snorted. "That it do—way beyond the means o' farmers like myself."

"So what would you say if I told you where you could get *free* fertilizer?" Carver grinned.

"You pullin' my leg, that what I say," said Jesse's father.

Carver laughed. "No, my good man. God has created all the fertilizer you need—free for the taking!—to feed these fields up here on this hill. That's where these little fellows come in." The professor dug into his pocket and held out a handful of small tan beans with a little black "eye."

"Them cowpeas?" Jesse asked curiously.

"Sure thing. Some folks call 'em black-eyed peas. But cowpeas, peanuts, soybeans—all the pod-bearing plants—have a wonderful secret." Carver's eyes danced playfully. "Most plants, like cotton, take nitrogen *out* of the soil. But beans and their relatives put nitrogen *back into* the soil! So if you rotate your crops—say, plant cowpeas or soybeans for two years in a row, plowing the stalks under after each harvest, *then* plant cotton, the cotton will have fresh nitrogen to feed on and give you more yield."

Cecil Turner's mouth was hanging open.

"Oh yes," Carver added, "about that free fertilizer." He pointed to the stands of oak trees that lined the road below. "Rotted oak leaves, covering the forest floor all around Bullock County. And swamp muck. You dig that up, spread it over your fields, plow it under—and manure, too. You folks got any animals?"

"Just Big Red here, a pig—an' my dog," offered Jesse.

"Hmm. A herd of cows would be better. But every little bit helps. You take care of this here mule, son? Let that manure dry out, crumble it up, spread it on your fields, plow it under—more free fertilizer."

Cecil Turner was staring at the lanky school teacher and rubbing his chin thoughtfully. "Say," he said. "Th' name's Turner—Cecil Turner. And this here's mah boy Jesse. Uh . . . would you mind comin' on by the house an' meet mah wife an' tell her what you been tellin' me? Ain't got much in the way of refreshment, but I'd like ta talk ta you some more."

"I'd be honored," said Carver. "Just let me get back to my wagon down there on the road, and I'll follow you home."

✧ ✧ ✧ ✧

"Cowpeas!" laughed Jenny Turner. "What we gonna do with cowpeas? Feed 'em to the hog?"

The Turner family was circled around Carver's funny-looking "School Wagon," as he called it, filled with jars and buckets of plants and trays of seedlings. "You could," smiled the professor. "But they make mighty tasty eating if you do 'em right. Would you mind if I showed you?"

Jenny looked at him uncertainly. "You mean . . . cook?"

Carver tilted his head modestly. "I'm a very good cook, if you don't mind me saying so. In fact, I've developed eighteen different ways to cook them, which I've written up in this bulletin here." He rummaged under his wagon seat and pulled out a thin paper booklet.

They had cowpeas and rice for supper that night, and Jesse thought he had never tasted anything so delicious—especially since he had worked up quite an appetite plowing under the old stalks on Sugar

Hill all that afternoon. As they ate, Carver talked. He explained again how having only one cash crop—cotton—was seriously hurting the farmers and their land. "You don't have much land, so you have to make the land you do have productive. Why, some crops have three, maybe four different uses."

"Don't foller yo' thinkin'," said Jesse's father.

"Well, take sweet potatoes. Now, there's a useful crop. Mighty good eating. But the vines and culls, when mixed with protein like corn, hay, or even molasses, make an excellent feed for stock. And if the potatoes are dried, you can keep 'em all year to make pies, laundry starch, yellow dye—even a coffee substitute."

Jenny Turner's eyes widened. "Don't say!"

"You see, my friends," Carver said, tapping the side of his head, "God gave us *minds* to unlock the secrets of nature! Everything we need God has put right here on the earth for us. And the more you can do for yourself, the less food and other goods you have to buy on credit at the local store. I call it 'living at home.'"

"Sho' do wish mah pappy could hear what you sayin', God rest his soul," murmured Cecil. Jesse glanced at his father—and saw something burning brightly in his father's eyes he had never seen before. "An' th' other colored folks round here. Most of 'em 'bout done lost hope."

George Carver nodded. "I know," he said gently. "That's why I take the School Wagon out into the back roads almost every weekend. If you would like to invite your neighbors to a demonstration tomorrow, I'd be happy to hold a class right here in your yard. But," he looked a little uncomfortable, "I don't mean to impose on your hospitality."

Jesse's mother and father looked at each other, then back at Carver. "Yes, yes!" said Jenny. "You be more than welcome—though we don't have much in th' way o' comforts."

"I'm a frugal man myself," Carver smiled. "Tell them ten o'clock tomorrow morning, then."

❖ ❖ ❖ ❖

Word spread among the sharecroppers and black farmers around Acorn like fire through dry tinder. By ten o'clock Saturday morning, the lane leading into the Turner yard was full of wagons, and Jesse was kept busy hauling water from the well to water the mules. Patch had to be shut up in the shed to keep from barking nonstop. Women as well as men came to hear the professor from Tuskegee.

The neighbors clustered around the School Wagon as Carver showed them sample cotton plants growing in buckets with two kinds of soil. One bucket contained soil from a field where only cotton had been grown for as long as anyone could remember; the other contained soil from a field that had rotated a crop of soybeans.

"Don't that beat all," said Thomas Tagoosa, looking at the hardy, thriving plant in the second bucket.

Carver talked to them about developing a "bal-

anced farm": "You can't eat cotton, so grow a bread-and-butter crop along with your cash crop. Most of you grow a little corn to feed yourselves and your animals. I would add to that a large vegetable garden with potatoes, tomatoes, greens, and squash."

"Cecil's hogpen don't leave no room for no vegetables," someone smirked. Everyone chuckled.

"Well, as long as you brought that up," said Carver, not missing a beat, "move that hogpen away from the house and the well. The privy, too. Animal and human waste shouldn't have a chance to leach into the water supply." He grinned. "Easier on the nose, too." Another laugh.

"I went for a walk early this morning, just thanking God for the beautiful world He has made. God loves beauty—have you noticed? I don't think God would take offense if we took a little pride in our farms . . . painted the buildings, planted some flowers."

Now the little crowd shuffled uncomfortably. Someone grumbled, "Takes money ta beauty up a place—money I ain't got."

Carver's eyes twinkled. "That's where you're wrong. Far as I know, God didn't spend any money when He created this world. Jesse—could you help me here?" The professor picked up a gunnysack. "Found some white clay over by that creek this morning. Jesse, sift the sand out."

Jesse shook the gunnysack, and sand rained out of the loose weave. Then Carver sent him to the well for water. The water and the sifted clay were mixed in a big iron pot Carver unhooked from the side of his wagon. "We'll let that stand a few minutes . . . let the rest of the sand and gravel sink to the bottom," he said.

After a few minutes Carver poured the "white water" in the pot into a clean flour sack that was sitting in another pot. "Keep dipping the sack till the clay is all dissolved," he told Jesse.

Jesse was enjoying himself as the center of attention. As he dipped the sack, he looked around the little crowd in their yard, grinning—but suddenly his grin faded.

Wayne and Udall Buck were leaning against one of the wagons, picking their teeth and watching.

What were *they* doing here? This was the first

time the Buck brothers had ever actually come into their yard—though most times those two acted like they owned the whole county.

"Jesse," said George Carver, "keep dipping."

Suddenly Wayne Buck's abrasive voice cut through the crowd. "Who you thinks you is, darky?" he challenged. "You insultin' us, comin' in here, tryin' to tell us farmers what ta do with yo' fancy ways."

An uneasy murmur shuffled through the gathered crowd.

George Carver pursed his lips thoughtfully, then said, "My apologies if I insulted you, sir. If what I am telling these farmers makes any sense, I invite you to try it and use it. If it doesn't make any sense, you will of course ignore it, and no harm done. Each man has the wisdom to decide for himself what is useful to him."

Jesse dipped furiously. Those two didn't deserve a civil answer.

"I think that whitewash is ready," Carver said, handing Jesse a big, fat paintbrush. "Would you like to do the honors?"

Jesse turned his back so he couldn't see the two white men, dipped the brush in the bucket of whitewash, and drew it over the gray, weathered pine boards on the front of their house. "Look at that," a woman murmured. "Gonna look like a new house."

"Friends!" Carver said. "I hope what you have learned today is that you can improve your farms even without money. But there is one thing that does cost money: land. And owning your own land is your ticket to dignity and well-being. How much does one acre of land cost?"

"Five dollars," growled Thomas Tagoosa. "Might as well be a hundred."

"I challenge you!" said Carver. "Grow your own food, don't waste anything that has some use . . . and save your cash to buy land!" He pulled a small coin out of his pocket. "See this nickel? If you saved a nickel every working day for one year, you would have enough to buy *three* acres of land and have fifty cents left over toward the next year."

A murmur of surprise rippled among the poor farmers. Jesse looked over at the wagon to see Wayne and Udall Buck's reaction.

But the Buck brothers were gone.

❖ ❖ ❖ ❖

The yard was empty. The front of the Turner home gleamed white and fresh in spite of the gaping holes between some of the boards. In some freshly dug dirt on either side of the front door sat a few small geraniums, which Carver had given to each farm wife.

Inside the cramped house, the Turners and their guest were eating another meal, this time of mashed cowpeas mixed with cornmeal and some of Carver's mysterious herbs, formed into a patty, and fried. Even Patch got one, wolfing it down in one gulp. But the dog turned his nose up at the green salad Carver had fixed with watercress from Shortcut Creek.

The day had had a holiday feel, marred only by the sulking presence of Wayne and Udall Buck. "Why you talk civil to them white trash?" Jesse wanted to know. "You got a hundred times more education. 'Sides, they stole our woodpile."

"An' busted the levee so it'd flood our field," piped up Willy.

"We don't know that for sure, Willy," said the boys' mother. Jesse kept quiet about his own suspicions.

Carver spoke gently. "Some people feel so inferior they have to dominate someone else to 'prove' they're superior to somebody. If I got upset every time an ignorant person insulted me, it would ruin my disposition and make me just as hateful as they are. That's one reason the Bible says to 'turn the other cheek.' God wants us to treat people like we want to be treated."

"You gonna preach at church tomorrow?" said Amanda shyly. "I heard Deacon Little ask you."

"I don't know about *preach*," Carver grinned. "I'm going to teach a Bible class—like I do up at Tuskegee Institute on Sunday nights. But I'm honored to be asked. You have some good neighbors, Turner."

" 'Cept those mean ol' Buck brothers," Jesse muttered under his breath. His mother gave him a sharp eye.

"But I worry about the sharecroppers—like your friend Thomas," Carver went on. "They're trapped in a system not much better than slavery and don't know how to get out. I admire you, Turner—you and your father. Wish I could have met him. To think that he hung on to these forty acres all these years—it's nothing short of a miracle. If you make use of the new methods I've been sharing with you, in five years this farm is going to be thriving."

Cecil Turner gave a strangled cry. Shocked, the four children stared at their father. "Cecil! What is it?" said his wife.

The big man put his head in his hands, and for a long moment, all they could hear was him sucking in air, as if he was having a hard time breathing. Finally he lowered his hands.

"Five years be too late," he said in a hollow voice. "I . . . I had to sign a note, put the farm up for collateral, else Harry Dickson wasn't gonna give me no more seed. If I can't pay off my debt *in full* right after harvest"—he looked up, his face stricken—"the farm be his."

Chapter 7

The Letter

PAPA DIDN'T HAVE NO RIGHT to do that!" Jesse told Big Red angrily, holding the bucket as the mule stuck his nose in and drank noisily. "Jus' as glad Grandpappy gone—would kill him all over again if he knowed what Papa done."

The news last night that Cecil Turner had signed a note, using their land as collateral in order to buy cottonseed, had stunned the whole family. Jesse's mother was the first one to find her voice. *"Well, now. Still might find a way to pay off the debt,"* she had said, trying to sound hopeful. *"Ain't no use cryin' over somethin' that ain't happened yet."*

But the news hung like a cloud over Jesse all during church the next morning. He had a hard time paying attention to Professor Carver's Bible class, even though the man seemed to know his Bible inside and out. Even the hot dishes of corn pudding, beans, and molasses the ladies of Mount Zion had prepared in Professor Carver's honor failed to dispel the gloom.

Now the family was back from church, and Professor Carver was getting ready to leave. After watering Big Red, Jesse slowly wandered back to where his father was helping Carver hitch up his wagon.

"Here, Turner, plant these," said the professor, hauling out two large sacks of cowpeas and setting them on the ground.

"I ain't takin' no charity," said Cecil Turner gruffly.

"Who said anything about charity?" Carver said. "I'm buying those two sacks of cottonseed you got, and this is my payment. Gonna take a while to enrich that soil up on Sugar Hill, but no time like the present to start."

The tall, slender man turned and stuck out his hand at Jesse. "Young man, I've got just two words for you: *plow deep*. Plow deeper than you've ever plowed before. It's harder work, but it pays off."

The rest of the family was gathering around the School Wagon. "Don't give up, my friends," Carver said, climbing up onto the wagon seat. "Remember what the psalmist said: 'I will lift up mine eyes unto the hills, from whence cometh my help. My help cometh from the Lord, which made heaven and earth.' "

He slapped the reins on his mule's rump. As the School Wagon rattled out of the yard, Carver turned on the seat and jabbed a finger in Jesse's direction. "Remember, son, plow deep!" he grinned. "Plow deep while the sluggards sleep!"

❖ ❖ ❖ ❖

Plowing deep was hard work. After a long day on Sugar Hill, Jesse's muscles ached from lifting the plow up at a steep angle so the blade would cut deeply into the soil. And plowing the dried stalks under didn't make it any easier.

He went to bed with Willy in the lean-to, but sleep didn't come. Part of Jesse felt excited when he thought about George Carver's visit and all the wonderful things the professor had taught them about making the farm more productive. At the same time he thought gloomily, *Why go to all that bother and hard work, only to have Mr. Dickson walk away with it come fall?*

Gradually the last lamp was blown out and the house quieted. Still Jesse could not sleep. Along with his aching muscles, he ached inside with the loss of his brother and grandfather. Funny, ever since the night Lee ran away and the levee broke, Papa had hardly said a word about Lee. Maybe because Papa knew he couldn't do a thing about bringing him back . . . Still, it was strange. And then Grandpappy dying . . . Jesse could hardly believe his grandpappy was gone. The last time he had talked to him was on the back of the wagon, when Grandpappy was talking crazy, something about wanting Jesse to have a sock—

Jesse sat upright on the straw tick in the lean-to. He'd forgotten all about Grandpappy's "sock." What was it Grandpappy had whispered to him? He had a sock he wanted to pass on to his grandchildren . . . but Lee was gone, so he wanted Jesse to have it . . . and it was for "th' land." But where? Where was the sock?

Jesse screwed up his eyes and tried to see the scene again in his mind. He'd been so worried about his grandfather that he hadn't paid a whole lot of attention to what the old man had said. *"A sock . . . 'neath a floorboard under mah bed"*—that was it!

Should he look for it now? Grandpappy's bed was just a narrow, rickety cot at one end of the "room" where the girls slept—an area defined by an old sheet strung across one end of the main room of the house. Could he find it in the dark? It'd make more sense to wait till morning—but Grandpappy had acted like it was a secret.

Crawling out of bed, Jesse opened the squeaky door of the lean-to and tiptoed across the main room, feeling his way past the rough plank table until his hand touched the room curtain. He pushed it back, listening to the breathing of his two sisters. Regular. Deep. Bumping into the end of Grandpappy's bed, Jesse dropped to his knees and felt underneath. What was he looking for?

His hand felt a broken floorboard, which left a

hole the size of a man's hand. He tugged at the broken piece, but it didn't budge. Gingerly he slid his hand into the hole, hoping against hope that no rat had built a nest under the floor. There. Something soft . . .

He drew it out. It was exactly what Grandpappy had said: a sock.

A sock with money in it. Money to buy more land.

✧ ✧ ✧ ✧

Jesse said nothing about Grandpappy's sock. After all, Grandpappy had given it to him to take care of. He hadn't been able to count it in the dark, but he knew it couldn't be very much—maybe ten, fifteen dollars in small coins, nickels and dimes. How long had Grandpappy been saving?

Jesse didn't know. He knew only one thing: Grandpappy had been saving to buy more land— land to pass on to his grandchildren.

The next day, as Jesse again followed Big Red back and forth behind the plow on Sugar Hill, a plan began to form in his mind.

Professor Carver's last words to him were *"Plow deep! Plow deep while the sluggards sleep!"* If he could get out to the fields *early* and do whatever farm chores he was supposed to do, maybe Papa would let him have a few hours in the afternoon to do odd jobs for shopkeepers in Acorn. Didn't Carver say if he could save a nickel a day, he'd have enough to buy three acres in just one year's time?

Papa didn't like the idea at all. "Get you a job? Now that Lee done take hisself off, I got enough work to keep yo' tail busy all day and all night, too! What you want a job for?"

But to Jesse's surprise, his mother supported the idea. "Now, Cecil. Jesse said he wouldn't neglect any of his reg'lar work. Manda and Willy and I can handle the vegetable garden—once Jesse plows us up a piece. And having a bit o' cash might come in handy, Cecil, you know it would."

It wasn't exactly Jesse's plan to fork over the money to his mother, but he figured now wasn't the time to tell her he wanted to save it.

To Jesse's even greater surprise, Harry Dickson liked the idea, too. "Well, now, I sure could use a boy to sweep out the store each afternoon," he said when Jesse slipped quickly past Wayne and Udall Buck, loitering on the porch of the Seed & Feed, and hunted up Mr. Dickson in the back stock room. "Hmm. You gettin' tall enough to stock those high shelves, too. All right. Tell you what. Every afternoon that you come in and give me an hour or two, I'll give you a nickel an hour. Give you some money for your pocket. Make you feel like a real man, eh?" Harry Dickson laughed and patted Jesse on the shoulder.

Jesse steeled himself and didn't flinch. Wouldn't do to offend his new employer.

✧ ✧ ✧ ✧

In spite of the debt they owed Mr. Dickson hang-

ing over their heads, Carver's visit had encouraged
the Turner family. Papa planted cowpeas in the
tired fields on Sugar Hill, moved the pigpen back

into the woods away from the house and the water well, and rebuilt the broken levee once Shortcut Creek was running more normally. Jesse plowed up a corner of the closest cotton field and part of the dirt yard for a vegetable garden and built a crude fence around it made of poles he hacked out of the pine and oak forest. Jenny Turner made the rounds of the neighbors and promised pies at wild berry picking time in exchange for a bit of this and a bit of that to start her vegetable garden.

And three or four times a week, Jesse took Big Red into Acorn to sweep out the Seed & Feed and to help Harry Dickson haul sacks of feed and stock shelves with dry goods.

The worst part of the job was running into Wayne and Udall Buck, who often sat on the porch with nothing better to do than make nuisances of themselves. "Now, Udall," Wayne said loudly enough for Jesse to hear the first week he worked for Mr. Dickson, "I sho' am s'prised that boy has 'nuff time ta farm hisself out. I'd-a thought his pappy be needin' him to chop a new stack o' wood, now, wouldn't you?"

"Har, har, har," cackled Udall. "I would at that." The two of them snorted and laughed.

Jesse seethed. One day . . . one of these days, he vowed, he'd get the best of the Buck brothers.

"Jesse, run over to the harness shop and pick up the mail," Mr. Dickson ordered one day. "Mr. Morris should be back from Union Springs by now." Matt Morris's combination harness repair and blacksmith shop and Harry Dickson's Seed & Feed were the two main "businesses" that made up Acorn, along with a tiny café that was closed more than it was open, and a sign outside a trim little house saying *Miss Lucy Shores* made fancy hats for "ladies." People who wanted to mail a letter left it at the Seed & Feed, and the next shopkeeper to go to Union Springs took it and picked up any mail for Acorn.

The harness shop was really a small barn and smelled of leather and sweat. Matt Morris was unloading boxes and small barrels from his wagon. He was built like a tree stump, with thick arms and legs and a crude manner. But for all his rough ways, he'd never said a mean word to Jesse.

"Th' mail?" he said. "Yeah, it's here ... somewhere." He rummaged in the wagon. "So you runnin' errands for Dickson now, boy? I could use a pair o' legs now & again if you can step snappy. Nickel a time. Deal?"

"Yessir, Mr. Morris, sir!" said Jesse, grinning.

"Oh, by the way, there's something for your pappy in that bunch o' mail."

A letter for Papa? Jesse's hand trembled with excitement as he took the batch of letters. Maybe it was from Uncle Howie ... or Lee! But he knew Mr. Dickson would have his hide if he saw him looking through the mail. He'd just have to wait till Mr. Dickson gave it to him to take to Papa.

"Here be the mail," Jesse said casually, laying the small stack on the counter of the Seed & Feed. He busied himself restacking some cans on a shelf, watching the store owner out of the corner of his eye.

To his surprise, Harry Dickson looked through the stack of letters without comment and laid it down again. Wasn't he going to give Jesse the letter for his father?

"Uh—'scuse me, Mr. Dickson," he said nervously. "I think Mr. Morris said there be a letter for my pappy in that mail."

"Oh . . . really?" said Mr. Dickson. He sounded annoyed. "Well, let's see here . . . oh yes, Cecil Turner. But since your pappy can't read or write, I'll just see what it is." To Jesse's astonishment, Harry Dickson opened up his pocketknife, slit open the envelope, and took out a sheet of paper. A flush of anger crept over Jesse's body. What *right* did that man have—white or not—reading his pappy's mail! He wanted to screech out, *"I can read it myself!"*—but he gritted his teeth together. Telling Dickson now would sound sassy. And Jesse knew the unspoken rules: colored folks who acted "smarty" around white people were "forgettin' their place."

Mr. Dickson glanced at the sheet of paper. "Mmm, sorry. Nothing personal. Just an advertisement. Don't think your pappy would be interested." He tossed it into a box of paper scraps and wood chips.

Jesse's anger dissolved in disappointment. So the letter wasn't from Lee or Uncle Howie after all. But . . . he was still curious. What kind of advertisement? And who sent it?

When Mr. Dickson wasn't looking, Jesse picked the paper out of the box and slid it into the waist of his britches. And that night at supper he brought it out and waved it gleefully in front of his family.

"Look, Papa! Look, Mama! Professor Carver done send us an in-vite to come up to Tuskegee and attend a 'Farmers' Institute'!" The family crowded around the sheet of paper. "Ever' month on the third Tuesday. And look a-here," Jesse went on proudly. "Carver done wrote us a note at the bottom! Says, 'Hope . . . you . . . can . . . come. . . . Bring . . . the . . . family. . . . G. Carver.' "

Chapter 8

Tuskegee

JESSE COULD HARDLY BELIEVE IT. Papa *and* Mama had agreed to make the thirty-mile trip up to Tuskegee in Macon County for the Farmers' Institute on the third Tuesday in July. They decided to leave on Monday afternoon (the flyer said families could "camp overnight") and come home the next evening.

It was the closest thing to a family holiday the Turner family had ever had. On the day of departure, Willy and Kitty danced in and out of the house, getting in the way until Mama finally threatened to leave them behind if they didn't "sit and shush!"

Jesse was excited, too—or he would be once they got past

Acorn. He dreaded passing the Buck brothers on the porch of the Seed & Feed, who would make it their business to know where the Turners were going. Papa was of the same mind. "I'd just as soon those two didn't know we be off the place for two days," he worried. But Thomas Tagoosa said he'd drop by to feed Patch and the hog on his way to chopping weeds in Harry Dickson's cotton fields.

To Jesse's relief, the chairs on the porch of the Seed & Feed were empty as Big Red walked briskly through Acorn pulling the Turner wagon. But Mr. Dickson came out of the store, wiping his hands on a piece of flour sacking.

"Hello, Cecil! Hello, Jenny," he hailed. "Where you folks off to?"

Papa was vague. "Howdy, Mr. Dickson. Headin' next county. Be back tomorrow." Jesse held the reins loose, and Big Red clopped on.

"Well, now, stop a minute," said Mr. Dickson. "I got somethin' for the young'uns to keep 'em occupied." He disappeared into the store, and Jesse had no choice but to holler, "Whoa."

Mr. Dickson returned with two sticks of candy.

Jesse tensed. Mr. Dickson used candy like fly paper.

Cecil Turner shook his head. "I can't put no more candy on my bill, Mr. Dickson . . . sir."

Harry Dickson beamed. "This one's on me, Cecil. Now, where was it you said you're goin'? Up to that Farmers' School in Tuskegee?"

Jesse knew his father wouldn't tell an outright lie.

"That be right," Cecil admitted.

"Well, now, that's a mighty long way to go, taking two days away from your farm . . . don't know that that's very wise, Cecil."

"We'll manage, sir," said Cecil stubbornly.

"Now, Cecil, I say this for your own good. We're a tight-knit community round Acorn. People don't like strangers comin' through, upsettin' things. I'd be careful if I were you, who you listen to. You don't want to put on airs, think you're better than the rest of the folks round here."

"I be careful," said Cecil flatly. "Chil'ren, say thank you for the candy to Mr. Dickson."

"Thank you, Mr. Dickson," Willy and Kitty chorused and waved good-bye as Jesse slapped the reins and Big Red jerked the wagon forward.

At last! They were off.

✧ ✧ ✧ ✧

It was nearly sundown by the time Big Red turned into the campus of Tuskegee Institute just outside the town of Tuskegee. The journey had taken about six hours under a relentless sun, with a few stops along the way to water and graze the mule. They had passed the train depot in Union Springs, and Mama had said wistfully, "Wish Lee would write, jus' let us know he all right."

The trip had been long and hot. But now, as they followed other wagons to a grassy spot in the shade of some large pine trees, Jesse could hardly sit still for excitement. Scattered all about the campus were large brick and frame buildings, some three or four stories tall. Across the road from the main campus were familiar fields of cotton. But between each cotton field other crops had been planted, most of which Jesse had never seen before.

Campfire rings had been built of stones so that each family could build a fire for cooking or washing up, and Institute students had filled a big barrel of water for the campers to use. After staking out Big Red with the other mules in a makeshift pasture, the Turner family ate a simple meal of boiled mush and cold sweet potato pie. While they were eating, a young man with close-cropped hair and golden brown skin, about Lee's age or a little older, came by to welcome them.

"Hello," he said, smiling warmly. "My name's Tom—I'm Professor Carver's assistant. If you'd like a tour of the school, meet me on the steps of Porter Hall—that wooden building on the hill—at nine o'clock tomorrow morning. After that, Professor Carver will meet us at the Slater-Armstrong Building to begin the meeting." Seeing their bewildered faces, he added, "The agriculture building, the new brick one over there." He beamed. "We students made the bricks and built the building ourselves!"

"Now, ain't that a wonder," said Mama when Tom moved on to the next family.

"Humph," said her husband. "Chil'ren of Israel had to make bricks, too, when they was slaves in Egypt. Thought gettin' an education was s'posed to mean our young'uns wouldn't have ta work so hard anymore."

Jesse was up with first light. It was fun sleeping under the wagon with Willy, with other campers all around. But it was strange having no chores to do, except take Big Red to the watering trough. To their surprise, Tom and some other students brought them eggs from the school's laying hens, and they had fried eggs and corn pone for breakfast. Jesse thought he'd never tasted anything as good as that fried egg.

About five of the camping families showed up for the tour. Most of the others had been to the Institute before. Tom pointed out the various buildings—classrooms, dormitories, the chapel—then took them to the various "industries" where students were hard at work. "Most of the students go home to help their families farm in the summer," Tom explained. "But some stay on and work at the school to help pay their tuition."

In one large shed, which Tom called the "foundry," a young man was tending two large fires in brick ovens, while several others were heating pieces of iron and forming them into farm tools and wagon wheels. In another, students were stitching shoes and tooling fancy designs on saddles.

"Look, Mama," Amanda gasped, "*girls* go to school here." They had stopped by classrooms with sewing machines where several young women were making dresses, shirts, and trousers. The twelve-year-old was even more impressed with the older girls and women who were weaving baskets, floor mats, and even women's bonnets from straw. "I didn't know you could take plain ol' straw and do that," she breathed, almost reverently.

They had to skip the sawmill, the tinsmithy, and the dairy because it was time for the Farmers' Institute to begin. New wagons had been rolling in all morning, and the meeting room in the "Ag" building seemed full of ordinary farmers and their wives, some with children. Most were black, but Jesse noticed at least two white farmers slip in and sit in the back.

Professor Carver began the meeting promptly at ten o'clock. Jesse was surprised to see him pick up a battered accordion and proceed to lead the farmers in several well-known hymns. This he followed with a Scripture reading from the Book of Psalms. Then he asked for "reports" from farmers who had been at the Institute before. "Anyone here from Hickory Grove?"

A middle-aged farmer with graying hair stood up. "We done like you tol' us las' fall and put ever'thing that rot into a compost pile—old newspaper, rags, leaves, grass, weeds, corn husks. You name it, we rotted it. Then we dug it into our vegetable garden, and them plants takin' over the whole place!"

"Good, good," said Carver. "Pinkston Crossing?"

Two families from Pinkston Crossing told about trying Carver's method of curing pork so they could butcher a hog in the spring and not have the meat spoil during the hot summer months. "We eatin' chitlins an' pork chops an' bacon an' salt pork in th'

middle o' *July*," said one farmer.

"Yep. An' we done like you said and split his hog fifty-fifty this spring, and we gonna split my hog fifty-fifty this fall," said the other. "Meat all year round and we each only butcher one pig!" The farmers clapped.

A farmer's wife from Liberty Hill said she planted parsnips, just like Carver had suggested, but she didn't care for the taste.

"What part did you eat?" Carver asked, a twinkle in his eye.

"Why, the greens," she said, surprised at his question.

"What did you do with the root?"

"Threw it away."

"Try the other way around," Carver suggested with a smile.

Jesse noticed that his mother listened carefully as Carver gave homemaking tips. "Seal jam with the white of an egg," he said. He encouraged them to not waste anything. "Don't throw out that grease; save it to make your own soap. Remember, everything you can make yourself saves money. And if you save your money, you can buy—"

"Land!" shouted the gleeful farmers.

Then came time for the topic of the day: insect pests. Carver had invited a number of the farmers to bring along any pests they'd found, which he proceeded to identify and give suggestions on how to control them. As the men and women crowded around Carver at the front of the meeting room, Jesse noticed three young men—were they farmers or students?—whispering among themselves in the back. Finally they wormed their way to his elbow.

"Professor Carver," said one, who had a confident air, "we heard you can identify jus' 'bout any bug there is." Carver just cocked an eyebrow. "Well, we found this strange bug—wondered if you could tell us what it be?"

Carver took the thin piece of bark the young man held out, to which a large bug was pinned with a sewing needle. The professor peered closely, frowned, turned the bark this way and that. Finally a small smile turned the corners of his mouth.

"Ah, yes," he said. "This is what we call . . . a humbug!"

The three young men looked at one another in astonishment, then burst out laughing. The bold one reached out and shook Carver's hand. "Everyone at the school brags about how much you know about nature. We thought, 'Nobody be *that* smart.' So we caught us some bugs, took 'em apart, and glued us a new one—thought you'd try to hoodwink us with some high-soundin' scientific name. But looks like you outsmarted us after all!"

✧ ✧ ✧ ✧

The day at Tuskegee passed all too quickly. The visiting farmers were fed a noon meal of bread made from soy flour, spread with something Carver called 'peanut butter,' which he'd made from peanuts, and dried apple slices that had been picked last fall. After lunch the farmers got a tour of the crops the school was growing, with another lecture on crop rotation. "Some plants are shallow feeders; others are deep feeders," Carver told them. "Each kind of plant takes something different out of the soil. Don't plant two shallow feeders two years in a row—alternate them with deep feeders."

All the way home Jesse thought about the school and all the farming experiments Professor Carver was doing. His whole body and mind felt alive like he'd never felt before. It was a new experience. He realized there were things to *know*, and even more amazing, *he* could learn them! When Carver explained things, they made sense.

Jesse had never had a goal, a purpose, before— not until he found Grandpappy's sock and decided to earn money to add to it, so that someday he could buy land. But now an even bigger goal seemed to be working its way under his skin and into his very soul.

He wanted to go to school at Tuskegee Institute and become the best farmer Bullock County had ever seen.

It was dark when Big Red turned off the road and into the lane leading up to their yard. Kitty and Willy were already asleep in the back. Jesse pulled the mule up next to the house, where Mama and Papa unloaded kids, blankets, food, and pots; then he led Big Red toward the shed. He could hear the hog rooting in its pen. *Good,* he thought, *hog's all right.*

Jesse was almost to the mule shed when he realized something was wrong. Where was Patch? Dog should have barked up a storm when they turned into the lane.

But as he unhitched Big Red, he heard whining from inside the shed. "There you are!" he said, unlatching the door. Patch nearly knocked him down with welcome kisses. "How'd you get yo'self shut in the shed?" he scolded, hugging the dog.

Jesse suddenly straightened. He shouldn't have been able to hear the hog in its pen—not since Papa had moved the pen almost to the woods. A quick run to the pole fence he'd built six weeks ago confirmed his fears.

"Mama! Papa!" he cried, dashing into the house. "Come quick! Somebody's done put the hog in the vegetable garden, and he's torn it all up!"

Chapter 9

The Broken Strap

THE HOG WAS HAPPY with his meal of fresh leafy vegetables, but the Turners were mad. "I thought Thomas was goin' to keep an eye on things!" Jesse stormed.

"I'm sure he did. But that don't mean he can be here ever' minute," said his mother. "But, sakes alive! Wonder how long that hog be in there! What he didn't eat, he trampled."

"What I want to know is how them Buck brothers knew we was gone?" sniffled Amanda. "Who else would do a mean thing like that?"

The mean trick had snatched the joy out of their holiday. While the rest of the family fussed and fumed,

Cecil Turner sat at the table, glaring at nothing in particular. Finally he muttered, "Maybe Mr. Dickson be right. Shoulda stayed home and taken care of mah own business, 'stead o' dreamin' big dreams. This farm ain't never gonna amount to nothin'. Don't matter how hard I work. They ain't gonna let us."

Jesse felt alarmed. He wanted his papa to fight back—or declare he wasn't going to let a couple of ignorant white trash get the best of *him*. But his father was acting like he was licked.

Well, Jesse wasn't licked. But it just wasn't fair that those good-for-nothing Buck brothers could get away with their meanness just because they were white.

Jesse was still thinking these thoughts when he went back to the Seed & Feed the next afternoon to do the sweeping after spending hours trying to salvage some of the vegetable garden.

"Sure could've used your help yesterday, boy," grumbled Mr. Dickson, handing him the broom. "Had to restock all those shelves myself."

Jesse considered. What was the right reply to that? Finally he decided on "Mighty sorry 'bout that, Mr. Dickson. I can stay late today if you need me to."

"Your trip worth all that time?" the storekeeper pressed. "Must've got home late—didn't see your wagon go by afore closing time."

"Trip was all right," said Jesse, sweeping his pile of dirt toward the front door. "Or woulda been, 'cept somebody—an' it don' take much to guess who—put our hog inside the vegetable garden and near tore it apart while we was gone." As soon as the words were out, Jesse could've bit his tongue. He hadn't meant to say anything. His mama had always warned him not to criticize white folks in front of other white folks.

"Now, now, who you blaming?" said Mr. Dickson sharply. "Easy to cast your troubles on someone else. You sure you didn't leave the hogpen open?"

Jesse swung the broom harder. He *knew* he hadn't left the hogpen open.

" 'Sides," Dickson continued, "even if somebody played a prank on you, it wouldn't have happened if your pappy had stayed home and tended his own business. He's got crops to raise and debts to pay and shouldn't be runnin' around the countryside thinkin' he somebody he ain't. No good gonna come of it." Mr. Dickson thumped the counter for emphasis.

Jesse's ears were burning. He could tell Mr. Dickson was looking at him, but he kept sweeping.

Mr. Dickson softened his tone. "Now, don't get me wrong, Jesse. Your pappy's a good man. We've been friends a long time. But he's stubborn—just like your grandpappy. But . . . you seem to have a good head on your shoulders, boy. Maybe you could encourage him to consider my offer 'bout sharecroppin'. He could wipe that debt clear, start over. Your family could stay on your homeplace—no problem with that. We'd be partners, like. And then—" he leaned over the counter and jabbed a finger at Jesse—"then if anybody messed with your property, they'd be messin' with *me*."

Jesse kept his eyes on the floor, still sweeping the clean floor. When he finally looked up, Mr. Dickson looked like he was expecting a reply.

"I'll tell Pappy what you said," he mumbled.

"Good boy!" Mr. Dickson beamed. "Now put that broom away and run over to Morris's shop an' ask him if my mule harness is ready. He's had it long enough."

Jesse was glad to escape out the door. Mr. Dickson made sharecropping sound like a good deal. But it didn't look so good when you saw how hard Thomas Tagoosa worked but never got anything out of it for himself. Mr. Dickson might cancel Papa's old debt in exchange for the forty acres, but Papa would always owe the man the biggest share of the crops.

The harness shop smelled good. Jesse looked around but didn't see Mr. Morris. But he heard iron clanging outside, so he went around back where the man was shoeing a big draft horse.

"What you want, boy?" the man huffed. "I ain't got no errands for you today."

"No, sir. I come for Mr. Dickson's mule harness, Mr. Morris."

The thick man lowered the hind leg of the horse and straightened up. "All right. I'm finished here. Let me look."

Jesse followed the man back into the shop and waited while he pawed around a pile of harnesses on a long workbench. Finally he held one up and looked at it. "Naw, it ain't done yet. But I'll do it now. Come back in half an hour." The man picked up a big knife, sliced off a piece of broken strap and tossed it on a scrap heap, then picked up a new length of leather.

Jesse turned away. Mr. Dickson hadn't said whether he should wait or not; he'd better go back to the store. He stepped out the door into the late afternoon sun—then suddenly drew back.

Wayne and Udall Buck were once again holding court on the chairs outside Dickson's Seed & Feed.

Jesse hesitated. He sure didn't want to walk by those two. He wasn't sure he could hold his tongue if they made some smart remark about the hog in the garden. But he had to get back to the store somehow.

Instead of walking across the dirt street to the front of the store, Jesse angled across to the empty café, slipped around back, and past the back of Miss Lucy Shores' house and hat shop. At the back of the Seed & Feed was a loading dock where people brought their cotton at harvest and picked up the heavy sacks of seed, flour, oats, or corn they purchased. He'd just slip in the back door; Mr. Dickson wouldn't mind.

But as he stepped onto the loading dock, he heard voices just inside the door—a woman was talking to Mr. Dickson.

"Look! Look at this letter from your father's lawyer." The woman sounded angry.

"I read it," said Mr. Dickson. "That's his job, Caroline, to remind me of the terms of my father's will."

Jesse pressed himself against the back of the store where he couldn't be seen from inside.

"This is no 'reminder,' Harry Dickson," hissed the woman. Jesse could hear paper rattling. "This is a *warning*. Read it! 'Item Two: All Dickson property taken away by the Union government and given away to slaves must be in Dickson possession by the year 1900, or ownership of the remaining property will pass from my eldest son, Harry Dickson, to be split equally among my remaining children.' That's only a year and a half away, Harry."

"I know what the will says," said Dickson, sounding annoyed. "And as you well know, Caroline, I have obtained almost all the original property owned by my father!"

"*Almost!* Almost isn't good enough, Harry! You don't have Cecil Turner's piece, and that forty acres could be our ruin."

Jesse felt like he'd been hit in the stomach. They were talking about the forty acres the government had given his grandpappy after the war!

"Calm down, Caroline," said her husband lightly. "Cecil Turner put up his farm as collateral against his debt to the store, to be paid in full after harvest. Don't worry. That last piece of land will be legally mine by this fall." There was a slight chuckle. "I'm makin' sure of it."

Jesse backed away from the door, then turned and ran along the backsides of Acorn's few houses and shops until he was out of sight of the Seed & Feed. Then he stopped and bent over, his hands on his knees, gasping for breath. He could hardly believe what he'd just heard! Dickson's old man—the man who had owned Grandpappy George back in slave days—wanted his land back, even though he was dead and gone now. No *wonder* Harry Dickson kept offering to cancel the Turners' debt in exchange for their land. No *wonder* he wouldn't give any more credit for seed after the levee flooded unless Papa put the land up for collateral.

Dickson *had* to get their land, or his father's will said he'd lose ownership of the rest of his property. Jesse wagged his head. Old Mr. Dickson must have been a bitter old man.

The boy straightened. But what had Mr. Dickson meant when he said that he was "makin' sure of it"?

Suddenly a wild idea split his thoughts, like a lightning bolt cutting through a stormy sky. Acting quickly, he darted back between the café and Miss Lucy Shores' hat shop and ran across the street. Slipping quietly into the harness shop, he casually made his way to the scrap heap where Mr. Morris had tossed that broken strap from Mr. Dickson's mule harness.

✧ ✧ ✧ ✧

It was hard to finish out his chores at the Seed & Feed, but Jesse did it. It was hard not to whip Big Red into a gallop on the way home, but he kept to a trot, feeling the mule's big muscles ripple under his legs as he rode bareback along the dirt lanes leading to the Turner farm. But when he got to the lane leading into their yard, he kicked Big Red and rode past, heading down the road toward Thomas Tagoosa's place. He could tell Big Red was confused. The mule wanted to go back to his shed, get a rub-down, and put his nose in a manger of hay.

But Jesse had something important to do.

He turned up the lane leading toward the levee and the ruined cotton field. When he got near the levee, he turned into the woods. Could he find it again . . . yes, there it was.

He slid off Big Red's back and knelt by the log that had been pulled out of the levee with the broken strap tied around it. Then he reached into the pocket of his overalls and pulled out the damaged strap he'd picked off the top of the scrap heap where Mr. Morris had tossed it after cutting it off Mr. Dickson's mule harness.

The two pieces fit together.

Jesse rocked back on his heels as the truth swept over him. It wasn't Wayne and Udall Buck who had pulled the log out of the levee. And it wasn't Lee.

It was *Harry Dickson*.

Chapter 10

The Swindle

HARRY DICKSON!" exploded Cecil Turner when Jesse ran into the house and spilled out the news. "Why would *he* do such a thing?"

"Jesse, you be sure?" asked his mother. "Wayne and Udall Buck be one thing, but Mr. Dickson . . ."

Jesse held out the muddy strap he'd removed from the log up by the levee and the piece he'd taken from Mr. Morris's scrap heap as proof. "See? A perfect match." Amanda, Willy, and Kitty crowded close to see. " 'Cause he want our land real bad, that why," said Jesse. And he told his parents about the conversation he'd overheard between Mr. Dickson and his wife.

Jenny Turner sank into a chair.

"If that don't beat all," she said. "So if Harry Dickson don't get our land by next year, the old plantation gets split up 'tween all his kinfolk?"

"That about it," said Jesse.

All the way home from the levee, Jesse had hardly known whether to be mad or glad. He was angry that Mr. Dickson had pretended to be their friend, angry that the most "upstanding citizen" of Acorn was really no different from the low-down, no-'count Buck brothers.

But he was glad—oh, so glad!—that it wasn't Lee who had pulled the log out of the levee. He hadn't realized how terrified he'd been to learn the truth, for fear it would turn out to be his own brother. Because if it was Lee, and his father found out, Jesse was afraid the fragile bond that held his family together would shatter. In such a hostile world, you needed to be able to count on your family.

But it wasn't Lee after all, and he had proof! Jesse had let out a whoop for joy on the lane going up to the homeplace and had spooked Big Red into a gallop right up to the door of the shed.

Jesse was startled out of his thoughts when his father suddenly banged the table with his fist. "I can't do this, Pappy!" Cecil Turner yelled, shaking his fist and looking up into the rafters of the ramshackle house. "You want me to hold on to this land, but I can't do it if the Bucks with they meanness and the Dicksons with they greed both determined to run me out!"

Kitty started to cry.

"Yes, you can, Cecil Turner," said his wife, leaping out of her chair and coming to his side. "It ain't Pappy you need to be talkin' to, but the Lord God. Manda, get me that Bible. 'Member that verse Professor Carver read that night he spend with us? Here . . . here it be. 'I can do all things through Christ which strengtheneth me.' " She looked at her husband, eyes blazing. "Who be bigger now? Harry Dickson . . . or the Lord God? Sho', you is angry. I'm angry, too. We gonna put that anger behind that plow and harvest us one big mess o' cowpeas, ain't that right, Jesse?"

Jesse's heart leaped. "That right, Papa! We got the cotton field *an'* the cowpeas still to harvest. Maybe we can still pay off that debt!"

"Me and the young'uns can pick cotton, Papa!" said Amanda, drawing herself up and suddenly looking a lot like her mama.

"Yeah, Papa, we help," said Willy. Kitty came close and hugged her father around his leg.

Cecil Turner's eyes glistened. He drew them all close in a fierce hug. "You right, you right. I been leanin' on myself. I got to lean on God, an' He give you all to me to lean on, too."

✧ ✧ ✧ ✧

The Turner family agreed among themselves to tell no one that it was Mr. Dickson who had flooded their cotton field, not even Thomas Tagoosa. Mr. Dickson had to think his plan was working, or else he might try something else—something even worse. "That especially mean keepin' yo' big mouth shut, Willy," Jesse said, keeping a close eye on his little brother any time they went into Acorn.

Jesse offered to quit his job at Dickson's Seed & Feed—in fact, he hated the thought of working for the man who was trying to cheat their family—but Mama and Papa were afraid Mr. Dickson might get suspicious if Jesse quit right now. So Papa and Jesse spent the rest of the summer chopping weeds, slopping the hog, collecting and spreading out Big Red's manure to dry for fertilizer, patrolling the levee to check for any trouble spots—man-made or nature-made. Mama and Amanda managed to salvage part of the vegetable garden, and a few more greens, green beans, tomatoes, and squash found their way onto their plates. Willy took over chopping wood and keeping the woodbox filled.

Three or four times a week Jesse went into Acorn to stock shelves and do general cleanup at the store. And every time he got two nickels, he gave one to Mama for the "nickel jar" to buy things at the Seed & Feed for cash; then, when no one was looking, he pulled up Grandpappy George's sock from under the broken floorboard and dropped in the other one.

Once the corn crop started coming in, Wayne and Udall Buck spent most of the summer in the woods making corn liquor in their still. When they did come into town, they were usually drunk. Jesse noticed that most of the white folks who came into town shook their heads and muttered comments about Wayne and Udall being a "public nuisance." Jesse didn't understand why Mr. Dickson let them sit in his chairs and never chased them off his porch. But then, there were a lot of things he didn't understand about Mr. Dickson.

The whole family picked cotton when the bolls were bursting with the big white tufts, filling bag after bag. But the harvest was still pitifully small from the fifteen tired acres planted in cotton. Mama rubbed their hands and arms with grease in the evening to soothe their raw fingers and sore muscles. And then she read the Bible to soothe their sore spirits.

And then they moved their picking sacks to the fields of cowpeas, which had put out a fair crop for the first year. The pods were easier to pick than cotton bolls, and the Turner family filled their sacks with hope.

In the late August evenings, as the din of the katydids swelled in the forest, they made plans how to collect dead leaves and swamp muck from the forest and plow them under with the plant roughage left behind after harvest. Next spring they'd plant cotton where cowpeas had been and cowpeas where cotton had been. George Carver had said they'd see a big difference next year.

If there was a next year.

✧ ✧ ✧ ✧

Big Red's ears twitched and his tail swished back and forth, back and forth, trying to rid himself of the pesky flies that swarmed around his sweaty hide as he stood in the line of wagons behind Dickson's Seed & Feed the last Saturday of August. Jesse and Papa sat on the wagon seat, not talking, waiting their turn as the cotton bales of one neighbor, then another, were hung by a hook, weighed, and paid for.

"Hello, Cecil. Hello, Jesse," said Mr. Dickson. "What y'all doin' back? I already weighed your cotton this morning."

"Cowpeas, Mr. Dickson," said Cecil. "Tryin' a new crop." He jerked a thumb to the big sacks of cowpeas in the back of the wagon.

Harry Dickson just stood on the loading dock, hands on his hips, shaking his head. "I *know* y'all planted cowpeas up on Sugar Hill," he said patiently. "But what I don't know is *why*, 'specially after you went in debt up to your nose to buy more cottonseed. Seemed like a dumb fool thing to do, but I figured you must have a powerful hunger for cowpeas, 'cause you know well as I do there ain't no *market* for cowpeas round here."

"New market gotta start somewhere with somebody," said Jesse's father, his voice even, his eyes looking straight ahead through Big Red's ears.

"Huh," snorted Mr. Dickson. "An' you think *you* are that somebody? Cecil Turner, that crazy George Carver has taken you for a fool. Cotton's the only cash crop round here. Always has been; always will be." He shrugged. "I'm sorry, Cecil, but I ain't gonna buy what I can't sell . . . move along, now. Next!" the storekeeper called out to the wagon behind them.

Jesse picked up the reins, and the wagon started to move as Big Red leaned into the harness. He looked at his father. Had they really expected Harry

Dickson to give them cash for their harvest of cowpeas? Not really . . . but they'd hoped.

"He right, you know," Papa muttered. "We gonna be eating cowpeas till we sick of they little black eyes." He glanced sideways at his son, and suddenly he snickered. Surprised, Jesse grinned. And then both their shoulders started to shake with silent, desperate laughter.

"Cecil! Wait!" someone called out. It was Mr. Dickson. The shopkeeper appeared beside the wagon, and Jesse pulled in on the reins. His father's laughter stopped as abruptly as it had started.

"Something funny, Cecil?" asked Mr. Dickson, frowning.

"No, sir, it ain't." There was no laughter in Cecil Turner's voice now.

"Well, there's no point in puttin' off what's got to be done. I'm calling in my note, Cecil. Come the first of September, I need payment of your debt in full."

"First of the—! Mr. Dickson, that be only next week."

"I know. No use draggin' this out. You can either pay or you can't."

"An' if I can't, Mr. Dickson?" Cecil Turner looked at the man eye to eye.

Mr. Dickson made a show of taking off his hat, wiping his perspiring face with a large blue handkerchief, and replacing his hat, avoiding Cecil's eyes. "If you can't, then we settle the debt with the land. Like you promised."

Jesse's father never took his eyes from Mr.

Dickson's face. "It ain't fair, Mr. Dickson," he said. Jesse thought Papa was almost on the verge of saying, "An' you know why." But he didn't.

Mr. Dickson still avoided looking at the father and son. "You signed a note, Cecil. Judge Barker comin' through Acorn Friday next, September second. We'll let him settle it." The storekeeper turned to go, then he turned back. "Your pappy's gone now, Cecil. Better this way. 'Member I said you could stay on in your place, sharecrop for me. Think about your family." Then he was gone.

Jesse let Big Red pick his own pace as they headed home. For a long while, neither father nor son spoke. Finally Jesse said, "What we gonna do, Papa?"

Cecil Turner narrowed his eyes with determination. "You gonna take this wagon o' cowpeas up to Tuskegee and ask Professor Carver can he help us sell 'em. Gotta be a market for 'em somewhere round here if he be telling farmers to rotate they crops."

"But, Papa—!"

"No buts," said his father. "I can't leave yo' mama and the young'uns alone . . . an' we don't dare all go away again or no tellin' what kind o' mischief take place. No, Jesse, you gotta do this. It be our only hope."

✧ ✧ ✧ ✧

Jesse left early the next day—Sunday—when the stores in Acorn were closed and no one saw him leave with Big Red and the wagon full of cowpeas. When he arrived at Tuskegee shortly after noon and asked for Professor Carver, he was told that the professor was out with the School Wagon—no one knew exactly where—but he should be back late that night.

Carver was surprised to see Jesse but listened thoughtfully to the boy's story. "It might take two, maybe three days, but we can find a buyer for those cowpeas," he said confidently. "How much cash does your father have to come up with?"

Jesse stared at him blankly. He didn't really know. He just knew that each year they hadn't been able to pay off Mr. Dickson fully, so the next year they were just that much more in debt. The debt at the store for seed, feed, and basic necessities had been slowly growing for years.

"Well, never mind. We'll do what we can do, and leave the rest in God's hands."

True to his word, Carver gave him the name of several different buyers in surrounding towns in Macon County. On Monday and Tuesday he had no success and returned to the Institute discouraged. Time was getting short. The first of September was Thursday. Even if he did find a buyer, was he going to get back on time?

But on Wednesday morning, a young man named O'Conner in nearby Chehaw, with red hair and freckles all over his face and arms, stroked his chin thoughtfully as he looked at the wagon full of cowpeas. "You say George over at the Institute sent you? Good man, George . . . I like some of his ideas. Alabama farmers are a thickheaded lot. Don't like change. But we gotta be open to change or we won't be ready for the twentieth century. Come on, drive that wagon over here. I'll give you a fair price."

Jesse didn't know what a fair price was. He just knew he was going home with an empty wagon and money in his pocket.

He could hardly wait to get home. Surely they'd be able to pay off the debt now! But he had to pace Big Red so the mule wouldn't wear out before they got to Acorn. It was almost dark by the time he pulled into the yard. Patch met him with joyful barks, dashing in and out of Big Red's legs.

"Mama! Papa!" he yelled gleefully. "I'm home!"

The sagging door of the house, its whitewash already wearing thin, swung open, spilling lamplight into the yard. A tall, thin figure was framed in the light. Jesse stared.

It was Lee.

Chapter 11

The Trial

JESSE JUST STARED AT HIS BROTHER, framed in the lighted doorway. He was so glad to see Lee, he wanted to leap off the wagon and throw his arms around him. But an awkward shyness kept him rooted to the wagon seat. And then a surge of resentment threatened to overshadow his relief. Where had Lee *been* for three months? Who did Lee think he was, running off like that, leaving him and Papa to—

"Come on," Lee said, stepping out of the doorway into the soft night. "I'll help you unhitch the wagon." He threw a glance into the empty wagon bed. "Sold them cowpeas? Papa will be mighty pleased."

Jesse let Lee unhitch the mule and turn him into the small pen beside the shed while he drew water from the well and poured it into Big Red's water trough. Neither boy spoke until the chores were finished; then Jesse swung himself up on the top rail of the pen and looked down at his big brother.

Lee absorbed Jesse's accusing gaze. "I know it was wrong, runnin' off like I did," he said, climbing up on the fence alongside Jesse. "I came home to 'pologize to Papa and Mama, try an' make it right."

"When—"

"Yesterday. Shoulda come before, but when Uncle Howie got the letter from Mama about Grand-pappy . . ." The older boy's voice choked up. After a few moments he said, "I couldn't face Papa after runnin' off like that an' not bein' here to help when the levee flooded. If I'd been here, maybe Grand-pappy . . ."

Jesse said nothing to ease his brother's guilt. Relief and resentment still played tug-of-war with his feelings. "So you been with Uncle Howie all this time?" he asked.

"Yeah. I caught up with him at Union Springs, tol' him Papa had changed his mind. So he bought me a ticket. Took me a while to pay him back. Uncle Howie got me a job at the factory where he works."

"You like it?"

Lee gave a little laugh. "Well, yeah, sorta. It be hard work, but at least you got cash in yo' pocket at the end o' the week." He looked at Jesse. "Papa tell me you been workin' sunup to sundown, tryin' to

116

hang on to this farm. I . . ." The older boy swallowed. "I guess I owe you a 'pology, too, leavin' you with all the work."

The last light of evening was fading. Jesse felt his resentment fading, too. "You back for good, Lee?"

Lee didn't answer. Instead, he said, "I guess Papa would like to know whether you sold them cowpeas or not. S'posed to go see Judge Barker tomorrow at the Seed & Feed at ten o'clock." He jumped off the fence and pulled Jesse off, too. "Ha! Guess ol' Dickson gonna get himself a surprise when we show up with the money, hey?"

The money! Jesse had almost forgotten about the money. Would it be enough? He'd better give it to Papa and Mama so they'd know where they stood before facing Harry Dickson tomorrow.

And then, as the two boys headed back to the house, Jesse had another troubling thought.

Now that his brother was back, did that mean Lee was the rightful owner of Grandpappy's sock?

❖ ❖ ❖ ❖

Mama and Papa counted and recounted the money from the cotton harvest and the crop of cowpeas. "Near as I can figure it," Mama said cautiously, "it just 'bout covers our debt at the store, with a little bit left over."

Jesse let out a whoop. Then he noticed that his father was silent. "Papa?" he said. "Ain't that good news?"

Cecil Turner nodded. "It be good news far as the debt. But . . ." He looked at his wife. "It sho' don't leave much to carry us through the year. An' I'm not sure Mr. Dickson gonna want to give us credit at the store if he don't get this land."

Once again Jenny Turner rose and went to her husband's side. "We worry 'bout that bridge when it time to cross it," she said firmly. "Professor Carver give us lots o' new ideas how to manage with what we got. Now, come on, ever'body get to bed. Whole family goin' to see the judge and wipe out that debt!"

❖ ❖ ❖ ❖

All the Turners knew about Judge Barker was that he was from Montgomery, Alabama, and he came to Union Springs, Acorn, Three Notch, and other small towns in Bullock County twice a year to handle small legal matters for folks who couldn't travel to the city. Jesse had imagined that the judge would be an older man with white hair and spectacles. So he was surprised to see a youngish man in his thirties with unruly dark hair and a big, bushy moustache, wearing a black suit and starched white collar, sitting behind Mr. Dickson's store counter, looking through some papers. Mr. Dickson was sitting on a chair in front of the counter, off to the right side.

The judge barely glanced up as the Turner family came through the door, and with a brief wave he motioned Jenny and Cecil Turner to sit down in two chairs to the left of the counter. Jesse, clutching a sack which he partially hid inside his overalls, stood with his brothers and sisters behind their parents. But a moment later the judge raised his head at a commotion at the door as Wayne and Udall Buck pushed their way into the store, saying something under their breath and guffawing.

"And *who* might you gentlemen be?" the judge asked coldly.

Wayne Buck stopped in mid-guffaw. "Why, I be Wayne Buck, Judge, and this here's mah baby brother." Udall Buck snickered. "We just comin' to this here trial as concerned citizens o' Acorn—ain't that right, Udall?"

"That right, big brother," squeeked Udall, giggling. Both the brothers reeked of corn liquor, even though it was only ten o'clock in the morning.

Judge Barker from Montgomery stood up. His dark eyebrows were pulled into a frown. "Let me get something straight," he snapped. "This is *not* a trial. No one has committed a crime. It is merely a hearing about a civil case, and—" he came around the counter, strode to the door, and opened it even wider—"the public is *not* invited. Good day, gentlemen!"

"Well—! Well—!" sputtered Wayne Buck. "Why, I never . . ." Judge Barker literally pushed the brothers outside and shut the door firmly.

Lee poked Jesse, but they dared not laugh.

"Now," said the judge, resuming his seat behind the counter. "I've been looking over your account here at the Seed & Feed, Mr. Turner. Unfortunately, even though you have made regular payments, the payments have not kept up with the amount of debt, which is considerable."

Jesse's eyes widened. The judge had called his father *Mr.* Turner. In his whole life he had never heard a white man address a colored man with the title of Mister. What did it mean?

"Now," the judge continued, picking up a sheet of paper, "I have here a handwritten note, drawn up by Mr. Dickson—" he gave a brief nod in Mr. Dickson's direction—"stating that forty acres registered in the name of George Turner . . . your father, I presume? . . . stating that these forty acres have been put up as collateral against this debt, which will be forfeited if you are unable to pay the debt *in full* after this year's harvest."

The judge looked up and handed the sheet across the counter. "Is this your signature—your mark— Mr. Turner?"

Jesse's father got up from his chair, looked at the paper, and nodded soberly. "Yes, sir. It is."

Judge Barker nodded. "Then there is only one relevant question before us this morning. Do you or do you not, Cecil Turner, have the amount in question to pay off this debt?"

Harry Dickson sat with his arms folded, his face passive, but Jesse caught a hint of a smile.

"I think I do," said Cecil Turner proudly, laying a small sugar sack on the counter.

The smug smile on Mr. Dickson's face disappeared, and his eyes narrowed.

The judge dumped out the contents of the sack—paper bills and coins—and began to count. He counted once, then he counted again. "Is this all?" he asked gently.

"A-all?" stuttered Cecil. "Y-yes, sir, that be all—but it should cover the debt an' a little over."

The judge pursed his lips. "Did no one explain to you, Mr. Turner, when you purchase things on credit, that the store owner is within his rights to charge you interest? This interest continues to accumulate on the portion of the debt that has not been paid."

Stunned, Cecil Turner looked back and forth between Judge Barker and Harry Dickson. Jesse heard his mother gasp, and his blood ran cold. The smug smile had returned to the storekeeper's face.

"The amount you have given me," said the judge, not unkindly, "does indeed cover the amount of the original purchases you have made at this store. But unfortunately, it does not cover the interest." He looked sympathetically at Jenny Turner and the children. "I'm sorry, but speaking legally, I'm afraid the farm is—"

"Wait!" shouted Jesse. Now his blood was boiling. He pushed past his brothers and sisters and stalked up to the counter. "That piece o' paper ain't legal! He *forced* Papa to sign it!"

"Now, wait a minute!" said Mr. Dickson, jumping out of his seat. "I did no such thing."

"Yes, you did!" Jesse shouted back. "This money be enough to pay off our debt *and* yo' stupid interest if the levee hadn't flooded an' make us buy more

seed. An' that flood weren't no act o' Mother Nature, either, Judge." Jesse pointed his finger directly at Mr. Dickson. "It was all *his* fault! *He* pulled a log out o' the levee an' *made* it flood! He wouldn't let Papa buy no more seed 'less he put the land up for collateral. An' it all his fault our grandpappy died tryin' to plug up the levee!"

Suddenly everyone in the room was talking and shouting at once.

"*Quiet!*" shouted the judge. Jesse's chest was heaving. The judge looked him square in the eyes. "Young man, these are very serious charges you're making. Think carefully, now. Do you have any proof?"

"I do," Jesse said angrily. He jerked the sack out from his overalls, reached inside, and pulled out the two pieces of the broken strap. "This one be the one we found on the log pulled out o' the levee," he said triumphantly. "An' this one be the one Mr. Morris, the harness maker, cut off Mr. Dickson's broken mule harness."

The judge took the two pieces of broken leather and fit them together thoughtfully. Then he said quietly, "But, son, can you *prove* this broken strap belonged to Mr. Dickson?"

Jesse opened his mouth, then shut it again. It was the same strap he saw Mr. Morris cut off Mr. Dickson's mule harness. But . . . suddenly he realized that he couldn't prove where he got it. He hadn't asked Mr. Morris for it. No one had seen him take it from the scrap pile. He was the only one who knew.

The judge's voice became hard. "These are very serious charges to make against a man of Mr. Dickson's reputation in this community *without proof*. I have no choice but to declare the Turner farm forfeit, to be turned over to Mr. Harry Dickson immedi—"

"Wait!" Jesse interrupted again, desperately. "How much more we owe for the interest?"

This time Judge Barker looked seriously irritated. But he said, "Sixteen dollars and thirty-five cents. Why?"

Jesse plunged his hand deep in his sack and pulled out Grandpappy George's bulging, lumpy sock. He turned the sock upside down and dumped its contents of coins all over the counter. "Count it, please?" he pleaded to the judge.

Jesse heard his mother gasp, "What?" The Turner

family all crowded around the counter. Jesse held his breath as the judge counted, making little piles of nickels on the counter. One pile . . . two piles . . . three . . .

Finally the judge looked up. He looked at Mr. Dickson. He looked at Jesse, then said, "Seventeen dollars and eighty-five cents." The judge stood up, picked up the piece of paper with Cecil Turner's mark, and tore it in half. "I think this debt is settled," he said. He counted out some of the coins on the counter and handed them back to Jesse. "Here. This is your change. Put it back in your . . . uh, sock."

❖ ❖ ❖ ❖

All the way home the Turners were giddy with excitement. Big Red seemed to catch the mood and moved along the rutted lanes at a good clip. Jesse told the whole story, how Grandpappy George had told him about the sock the night he died, how he wanted to leave an inheritance for his grandchildren. "He said it was for the land," Jesse said. "I know he meant he was savin' to buy more land, so I jus' kept adding nickels to the sock—like Professor Carver said. It wasn't a nickel a day, but . . ."

"You mean some o' that money you gave the judge to pay off Mr. Dickson was money Mr. Dickson paid you?" Lee asked, slapping his knee. "Don't that beat all!"

Jesse looked at Lee. "Yes, but . . . that sock was s'posed to be yours, Lee. Woulda been if you hadn't

124

run off. I guess I jus' spent yo' inheritance."

Lee wagged his head. "I think Grandpappy woulda done the same thing, Jesse. It went for the land, didn't it? 'Sides, I plan to head on back to Philadelphia someday—wait, wait, Mama. I don't mean now. 'Cause I been thinkin'. I got some makin' up to do with this family. What I think is ... it be Jesse wants to farm this land. So I think Jesse ought to get himself up to that school in Tuskegee and learn how to do it right. An' I'll stay here an' farm with you, Papa, till he done. That a promise."

Jesse could hardly believe his ears. Go to Tuskegee Institute? Would his brother really do that—help Papa on the farm so he could go? He'd have to stay at Tuskegee and work summers to pay his school fees, but if Lee was serious ...

Jesse felt a flood of gratefulness toward his big brother. But there was something he still didn't understand. When he had a chance to be alone with Lee, he brought it up.

"Lee, uh ... something I've been meanin' to ask you. When I went out to hitch up the wagon the night the levee broke, Big Red was wet and muddy. I *know* I rubbed him down the night before. So it looked mighty suspi—"

"Oh! That!" Lee laughed easily. "I took Big Red, thinkin' that was the only way I could catch up to Uncle Howie. Was jus' gonna leave him in Union Springs; figured Papa would get him back somehow. But half mile down the road, I realized I couldn't do it—not leave an' take Big Red, too. So I brung him back, then set off on foot. No harm done, right?" But suddenly Lee looked alarmed. "What you mean, it looked 'suspicious'? Jesse! You and Papa didn't think *I* pulled that log out o' that levee, did you? All this time—!"

Jesse shook his head and smiled. "Never tol' Papa. Glad I didn't."

Chapter 12

Epilogue: 1904

JESSE CRANED HIS NECK to look past the rows of graduating students, trying to locate his parents. There. Sitting in the second row of the section reserved for families. Papa looked uncomfortable in his starched shirt collar and suit coat, but Jesse thought Mama looked mighty fine in the pretty green dress she'd made. And Amanda! Almost looking like Mama's twin now that she was eighteen. His sister was wearing a straw bonnet she'd made herself—one of the many styles she'd designed and started selling to other black folks around Acorn who couldn't afford the likes of Miss Lucy Shores' hats.

He craned his neck again, trying to find Lee and the young'uns, but his search was interrupted by the speaker on the platform who was saying, ". . . and now, the president of Tuskegee Institute, Booker Tiaferro Washington."

The graduating students seated at the front of the Pavilion stood and began clapping, followed by their families, townspeople, and other visitors. The distinguished-looking man who came to the podium accepted the applause graciously and motioned to the people to sit down.

"Thank you," said President Washington. "On behalf of the entire faculty and staff of Tuskegee Institute, I want to welcome all of you to . . ."

Even though he'd heard Booker T. Washington speak on several occasions, Jesse was always amazed at the man's powerful speaking voice. It carried clear to the back of the Pavilion and commanded everyone's attention—not at all like Professor Carver's soft tenor, which tended to squeak if he tried to speak loudly. Washington, who was not yet fifty, cut a fine figure with his trim moustache and dark, brooding eyes.

"You have a responsibility!" he was saying, fixing the graduates with his intense gaze. "Your education will be worthless if it stays locked up in your head. An ounce of application is worth a ton of abstraction! *Use* what you have learned during your years at this Institute to better yourself and your neighbor. Never refuse to lend a helping hand to your fellowman—no matter what color or station in life."

From past experience, Jesse knew the president's speech would become stronger and more passionate.

"Whatever you put your hand to, do it well. No race can prosper till it learns that there is as much dignity in tilling a field as in writing a poem."

Jesse winced. He couldn't imagine writing a poem! It had taken him six years as it was to get through Tuskegee's vocational program, which included basic reading, writing, and math, along with the practical skills of farming, which was his real interest. He'd heard that there were Negro colleges where students studied literature, music, history, French, and Greek (so they could study the Bible). And he had heard Papa and Uncle Howie arguing about what kind of education was best for the Negro race. Jesse supposed both were important. But for himself, he liked learning things that would help him earn his own living, skills that helped him do what had to be done in the best possible way.

"Do not lose heart when you face injustice," Washington continued. "Be patient. By our very perseverance we will earn the respect of our fellowman. Every day we have a choice on how to view the world: Is our cup half full or half empty? We should never permit our grievances to overshadow our opportunities!"

The president's speech was over. The crowd rose and gave him a standing ovation. Jesse noticed that some of the white people in attendance clapped with special enthusiasm.

The graduates were being called forward to receive their certificates. "Buck Anderson, Wheelwright . . . Joe Carter, Blacksmith . . . Jewel Jones, Dressmaking . . ." And so it went through the alpha-

bet, until finally Jesse heard: "Jesse Turner, Agriculture." Jesse's heart thudded in his chest as he walked across the platform. He hoped he wouldn't trip over his own feet and make a fool of himself. But he managed to shake President Washington's hand, and he couldn't help grinning when he saw his name on the official-looking certificate with its gold seal.

As he walked off the platform, he glanced down to where his father and mother were sitting in the second row, smiling proudly. And just behind them he caught Lee's eye; he was grinning and jerking his thumb at the man sitting next to him. Jesse's mouth fell open in surprise.

It was Uncle Howie!

❖ ❖ ❖ ❖

The whole Turner family nearly smothered Jesse when the graduation ceremony was over and they found each other outside the Pavilion. "Uncle Howie!" Jesse said when he finally peeled himself away from eleven-year-old Kitty's excited hugs. "When did you get here? I wasn't expectin' to see you!"

In spite of the early-June heat, Uncle Howie looked sharp and cool in his wheat-colored suit and crimson tie. "Couldn't miss the graduation of my nephew, now, could I!" Howie grinned. "I'm proud of you, son, right proud."

"What you think of Booker T's speech, Howie?" said Papa, slapping his brother on the back. "And did you see them white politicians from Washington? They respect our Booker T. up there in Washington, D.C."

Uncle Howie nodded in cautious agreement. "I imagine they liked that speech right fine. White folks like Booker T. 'cause he careful to tell colored folks to do all they can to better themselves, but he just as careful not to tell white folks what *they* need to do so we can."

"What you mean, Uncle Howie?" spoke up Willie, who was a strapping fifteen-year-old now.

"Waal, young man, don't s'pose you've noticed that here in Alabama even an important man like

Booker T. Washington can't vote?"

"Now, Howie," broke in Jenny Turner, "these things take time."

"Time?" Howie gave a short laugh. "Guess they do, since it's already been thirty-five years since Congress passed the Fourteenth and Fifteenth Amendments giving *all* men born in the United States the right to vote, regardless of race. An' things getting' worse 'stead of better. Jim Crow laws poppin' up all over the South sayin' colored folks can't eat here, can't drink that, gotta ride somewhere else—"

"Now, now," broke in Jesse's mother. "Let's not spoil this special day arguin' 'bout politics. Jesse, didn't you say you wanted to show us Professor Carver's laboratory?"

Jesse was kind of sorry Mama had changed the subject. He knew Uncle Howie was right about things getting worse. It seemed the harder black folks worked to improve themselves, the madder some white folks got about it, figuring out new ways to keep Negroes "in their place." On the other hand, he truly respected President Washington and Professor Carver, who often said that if he got upset every time he experienced injustice, he'd have no time left for his work.

But Jesse *was* eager to show his family the laboratory. He led them into the cool silence of the Slater-Armstrong Building, where Carver had his lab. "Mama, look at these beautiful paintings!" said Amanda as they entered, noticing the framed artwork of delicate flowers hanging all around the laboratory.

"Thank you, missy." Startled, the family turned at the sound of the familiar voice. They hadn't seen Professor Carver working quietly at a worktable in the corner of his laboratory.

"You painted these, Professor Carver?" asked Jenny Turner in amazement. "They are magnificent! Why didn't you pursue art as yo' career?"

George Carver joined the family group, wiping his hands on his lab apron. "Because I felt I could be of more service to my race in agriculture," he said simply. "Come on over here. I'd like to show you something."

Crowded on a worktable was a whole display of different kinds of items—a bottle of ink, a jar of rubbing oil, a sack of meal, a jar of cooking oil, a box of washing powder, a can of polish, and a lot of things none of them recognized.

"What's this, Professor Carver?" Kitty was holding up a container of black gunk.

"Axle grease, to keep your wagon wheels turning smoothly," he grinned.

"What's all this different stuff for?" asked Willie, playing with some flexible flooring.

Carver cocked an eyebrow slyly. "All these different products have something in common—they're all made from the peanut."

"Peanuts!" Cecil Turner's jaw dropped. "Those lil' goobers kids like to eat?"

"The same." Carver grinned. "That, dear friends, is the nature of my work—to discover the secrets the Creator has locked inside His creation to benefit mankind." He turned to Jesse. "Jesse, congratulations. You've been one of my best students. But I have one last word for you: Never stop learning! And what you learn, share with others. Remember, the more ignorant we are, the less use God has for us."

❖ ❖ ❖ ❖

Jesse gave a sigh of contentment as he sat on the patchwork blanket his mother had spread on the grass on the front campus. The picnic lunch of chicken, beans, and corn bread had disappeared. Other picnickers were laughing and eating all over the thick green lawn that had been just dry, dusty dirt when Jesse first came to the Institute.

It was almost time to harness up Big Red and go home. Jesse was excited to get back to the farm—though it would be hard when no Patch came out to greet him, smiling his doggy smile and wiggling all over. Papa had said that Patch disappeared one day, and Thomas Tagoosa had found his body back in the woods. Thomas thought the dog had been poisoned.

The Turners still had enemies in Bullock County.

". . . comin' back to Acorn with us, Howie?" Mama was saying.

"I'd surely love to, Jenny," said Uncle Howie. "But I've got to get back to Philadelphia. Man named DuBois and others have formed a group called the Niagara Movement, doing what they can to demand our right to vote in this country."

"Papa, I'd . . . I'd like to go with him," Lee said

suddenly. "I've kept my promise, worked the farm till Jesse graduated. But I'm twenty-three now. Gotta make my own way. Besides, Jesse's worth two of me with all the learnin' he's got in his noggin. . . ." Lee playfully punched his brother in the shoulder and grinned. "Far as I'm concerned, lil' brother, you can *have* the farm now."

Jesse looked at Lee with a pang of sadness. How could he ever thank his brother for helping him get a head start on his dream . . . on Grandpappy George's dream . . . to work his own land and be self-sufficient? But Lee was right—he had to go his own way.

Jesse looked at his father and Uncle Howie . . . then at Lee and himself . . . and realized two sets of brothers were going two different directions. But suddenly Jesse understood something. They weren't opposite directions.

It was going to take both kinds of effort—the "practical" folks like George Washington Carver who try to work within the system, and the "activists" who try to change it—to move their people forward.

More About
George Washington Carver

IN 1860, NIGHT RAIDERS rode into a farm near Diamond Grove, Missouri, and stole a slave woman and her baby, hoping to make a profit reselling them in the South. Moses Carver, who had bought the young woman as a companion for his wife, offered one of his prize racehorses for their safe return. A bounty hunter took up the chase but returned with only the sickly baby. Moses Carver gave him the racehorse anyway.

Little George, as he was called, and his older brother, Jim, were raised by Moses Carver and his wife as foster sons. Too frail for heavy farm work, George developed a deep love for God's created world. He also had a boundless curiosity: Why did flowers grow here and not there? What else could you do with sweet potatoes besides eat them? Why did some crops seem to wear out the soil they were planted in? All growing things seemed to have secrets locked inside—and George was determined to find the key.

But first he had to learn to read. The local school would not enroll "colored" children, but George was determined. At fourteen years of age, he left home, intent on getting an education wherever he could find it. He worked odd jobs in towns all over Missouri and Kansas, going to school wherever they would let him in. His first "textbook" was a Bible, and he developed a habit of daily Bible reading that gave him direction and strength the rest of his life.

When he had learned all a teacher had to teach, he moved on, supporting himself by learning to cook and taking in laundry. Early on he developed a philosophy that so much work was worth so much pay, and he would not take charity.

At the encouragement of some white friends, Carver applied to Highland College in Kansas. His heart filled with joy when he received an acceptance letter. But when he showed up on campus and presented his letter of acceptance, the dean frowned. "You didn't tell us you were a Negro. Highland College doesn't take Negroes."

Carver was devastated. There was so much more to learn! He walked away, discouraged by racism that looked at a man's skin color rather than his heart and mind.

But Carver did not cease to learn. He taught himself to paint pictures and play the accordion. In

1888, he gathered his courage once more and applied to Simpson College in Iowa—only the second black person in the college's history. He loved art, and astounded many with his beautiful paintings of flowers. But at his art teacher's urging, he transferred to the Iowa State College of Agriculture and Mechanic Arts in Ames, Iowa, to study horticulture, eventually earning a master's degree in agriculture and bacterial botany.

Iowa State wanted George Carver to stay and teach, but he was restless. What was God's purpose for his life? God had given him so much; how could he "give back what he'd been given" to help his own people? The answer came in a letter from Booker T. Washington, a prominent black educator, who wanted him to head up the new Agriculture Department at Tuskegee Institute in Tuskegee, Alabama. George Carver packed his bags.

He arrived on Tuskegee's campus on October 8, 1896, and began with thirteen students in his two-year program. By spring of the following year, he had seventy-six students! That same spring of 1897, the Tuskegee Experiment Station was established on campus. Carver and his students experimented with ways to conserve the soil, introduce new crops to help break the stranglehold of "King Cotton," be more self-sufficient, and develop new uses for farm crops to help create a bigger market. The results were published in a bulletin and distributed to surrounding counties—but what about the farmers who couldn't read?

Carver believed that "demonstration" was the purest form of teaching. People needed to see and touch. He developed two strategies to help local farmers: One was a monthly "Farmers' Institute" on the campus of Tuskegee, where farmers could come and see the various farm experiments, ask questions, and discuss their problems. The second strategy was a "traveling school" on weekends. Carver and an assistant would load up a farm wagon with samples and demonstration materials, and travel the back roads of Alabama to reach the poorest farmers with practical ways to improve their farms, their families, their lives.

By the time the sun rose each day, Carver was already out walking in the woods for prayer. His favorite Bible passage was Psalm 121:1–2: "I will lift up mine eyes unto the hills, from whence cometh my help. My help cometh from the LORD, which made heaven and earth." The students recognized the source of his wisdom and asked him to lead a weekly Bible study, which by 1911 was attended by a hundred students.

Carver was a demanding teacher. "Don't tell me it's *about* right," he'd say to a student who had just given him an inexact answer. "*About* right might as well be wrong." And then he'd say, "If you come to a stream that's five feet wide, and you jump four and a half feet, well, that's *about* right. But you might as well just topple in at the near bank and save yourself the effort."

Around the turn of the century, there was a lot of

controversy about what kind of education and social efforts would most advance the black race in America. On one hand, W. E. B. DuBois believed that blacks should *demand* their full rights as citizens, including the right to vote and a classical higher education emphasizing literature, languages, and the arts. On the other hand, Booker T. Washington counseled patience and courtesy in those demands, concentrating on vocational training so that blacks could be self-supporting, becoming businessmen and property owners, a philosophy of "conciliation" he thought would earn respect and eventually full civil rights.

George Washington Carver refused to get involved in controversy about race or else he would have no time left for his work. But his improvements in agriculture were gradually noticed by other institutions and government officials, who asked him to lecture or give demonstrations. These invitations were bittersweet; as a black man, he was often treated as a second-class citizen, then given high praise as a scientist. But Carver believed that self-pity was a destructive force. He accepted in silence the personal injustices that came his way because he knew that to dwell upon them in his mind would drain him of energy he believed might be put to better use.

But he occasionally had a sharp word of insight for any willing to listen. "Your actions speak so loud I cannot hear what you are saying. You have too much religion and not enough Christianity—too many creeds and not enough performance. This world is perishing for kindness." Another time, explaining why a white person said something hurtful, he said, "[S]he . . . was afflicted with a feeling of being inferior, which forced her to dominate somebody to prove she was superior."

During his lifetime, George Carver dedicated his knowledge of science to helping the common man make a living. He developed 200 new products from the peanut, and 118 practical products from the sweet potato, creating new markets and expanding the number of commercial crops. In so doing, he broke King Cotton's grip on the South, renewing the tired soil and benefiting whites and blacks alike.

A brilliant man, George Carver remained humble in spirit and always gave glory to God for his achievements. When he died in 1943, his epitaph read: *He could have added fortune to fame, but caring for neither, he found happiness and honor in helping the world.*

For Further Reading . . .

Carver, George Washington; Kremer, Gary R. (editor); Kremer, George Washington. *George Washington Carver: In His Own Words.* University of Missouri Press: Columbia, MO, reprint edition 1991.

Holt, Rackham. *George Washington Carver: An American Biography.* Doubleday & Company, Inc.: Garden City, New York, 1943, 1963.

Moore, Eva. *The Story of George Washington Carver.* Scholastic Biography: New York, reissue 1995.

Wellman, Sam. *George Washington Carver: Inventor and*

Naturalist. Heroes of Faith series. Barbour & Co.: Uhrichsville, OH, 1998.

"I love the TRAILBLAZER BOOKS. I can't wait to read them all!"

— Josiah, ND

Have *you* read them all? Here is a sneak peek at another TRAILBLAZER BOOK you don't want to miss!

The Bandit of Ashley Downs

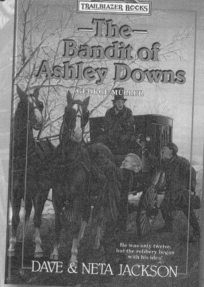

Twelve-year-old Curly is an orphan, acrobat, and master pickpocket. When he overhears that a church is raising money for an orphan house, he plans an armed robbery that promises to bring him enough money for a lifetime.

But is Curly in for more trouble than he bargained for? If he is caught, which fate would be scarier—to be sent to prison, or to the very orphanage from which he stole the money? Would George Müller, the man in charge of the orphanage, make Curly into a slave to earn back at least a portion of the money? Or might they do something even worse?

Curly is in for the biggest surprise of his young life!

For a complete listing of TRAILBLAZER BOOKS, see page 2!

❖ ❖

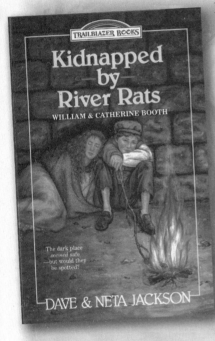